Starve Acre

Also by Andrew Michael Hurley

The Loney
Devil's Day

Starve Acre

Andrew Michael Hurley

JOHN MURRAY

First published in Great Britain in 2019 by Dead Ink Books

This edition first published in 2019 by John Murray (Publishers)
An Hachette UK company

1

A CIP catalogue record for this title is available from the British Library

Hardback ISBN 9781529387261
eBook ISBN 9781529387278

Typeset in Baskerville by Hewer Text UK Ltd, Edinburgh
Printed and bound in Great Britain by Clays Ltd, Elcograf S.p.A.

John Murray policy is to use papers that are natural, renewable
and recyclable products and made from wood grown in sustainable
forests. The logging and manufacturing processes are expected to
conform to the environmental regulations of the country of origin.

John Murray (Publishers)
Carmelite House
50 Victoria Embankment
London EC4Y 0DZ

www.johnmurray.co.uk

For Glenn and Paula

'That is a quiet place –
That house in the trees with the shady lawn.'
'– If, child, you knew what there goes on
You would not call it a quiet place.
Why, a phantom abides there, the last of its race,
And a brain spins there till dawn.'

Thomas Hardy, 'The House of Silence'

The Raker-of-Mud
The Hot-Footed-One.
Jolly-Night-Drunk.
Earth-on-the-Run.

Piece-o-the-Dark.
Lugs-in-the-Hay
The Owd Duke-o-March.
The Jester-o-May

Twitch-in-the-Bracken
Dandelion Jack
Eyes-all-a-startle
Marker-of-Tracks

Earth-Thumper.
Witch-Puppet.
Lurker-at-Dusk
'Tis part of his game
To vary his name.

'The Hare', a folk song

Part One

Overnight, snow had fallen thickly again in Croftendale and now in the morning the fells on the other side of the valley were pure white against the sky. Further down, where the sun had not yet reached, the wood by the beck was steeped in shadow and would stay cold all day. The freezing mist that was twined between the leafless beech and birch had already driven a hungry fox to seek food elsewhere. A line of deep paw prints came out of the gloom and into the pearly light that washed over the drifts on this side of the dale. Yet the animal seemed to have changed direction abruptly; startled into a hollow or a ditch by the folk out shooting nearby – men from Micklebrow, probably, who'd walked over the moor to take advantage of the wide empty canvas on which the grouse and pheasants were as bright as streaks of paint. The sound of shotguns and whistles doubled in air that was uncannily still and expectant after the blizzard. The storm had lasted for hours and the extent of its fury was marked by icy cornices blown over the dry-stone walls. They were wild jagged crests, like those of a sea surge breaking on inadequate defences.

So the winter went on. Adding to itself day by day. Making the houses in the dale seem even more remote from one another than usual.

None of the farmers had been out yet with a plough and on the road by Starve Acre the snow cleared the evening before had frozen solid. All along the verges it was piled like crumbled pieces of cumulus.

From his study, Richard Willoughby heard another volley of gunfire and watched the rooks burst from the ash trees outside the window. They scattered in a mess of wings and curses and flapped away to the field across the lane. For days now, they had gone foraging in the frosted hummocks there out of desperation and had found little or nothing in the way of sustenance.

It seemed to Richard that February simply refused to leave the dale. He wished that it would and soon. There was something about being able to say that it was March. Something in the name that suggested energetic purpose and the onward movement of things. A time to work. A time to shoulder the yoke. There were lines of poetry about the early spring that he thought he should like to learn as reassurances that the world would turn green again. On a day like this, it was easy to have doubts. Everything was starving and puny. Everything was waiting, just as he was.

The rooks spun in the sky, their calls cracking on the frozen air and, as he watched them, Richard felt a swelling sensation in his head – something akin to the start of a migraine.

He blamed himself for getting distracted. When he was in the study, he was normally so attentive to his work (devoid of family photographs, it was his oubliette), but Ewan could find him in the strangest of ways.

The rooks reminded him of the paper birds he'd once made in the small hours when the boy had been frightened and restless. And how, when the birds had been folded into shape, he'd told stories with them and Ewan had eventually gone, his big eyes closing in much needed sleep.

Richard left the sentence he'd been mulling over half typed, moved to the armchair next to the bookshelves and switched on the radio. One of the Brandenburg Concertos was in full flow. He put on his headphones and turned up the volume until the strings and horns were distorted, trying to lose himself in the noise and banish Ewan to the dark hole from which he had emerged. If he had to be absent, then why couldn't he remain so? A blank could be coped with, just as a man might become used to a missing hand or foot and improvise a way of living until it became habit and habit a kind of normality.

After the funeral at the end of the previous summer, Richard's tactic, just as it was now, had been to work as hard as he could – so that when the new academic year began he'd turned apian, darting from one thing to another but giving each new task his full devotion.

Perhaps he had been naïve to expect people not to treat him any differently but their insistence on doing so became frustrating and his colleagues in History had quickly learned that if they approached him with a look of sympathy he would avoid them.

He had never been pitied before. He found the attention unbearable. Can't stop, he'd say, or, running late. And if they persisted anyway, walking with him across campus, then he ensured that conversation turned to some work-related matter. Work was all he talked about. Work was all he did. Before lectures, he would ensconce himself in the depths of the library and return after he'd finished teaching for the day. He'd attend every meeting, even those that didn't directly concern him. He'd come in early to prep; he'd stay late for tutorials with his Masters students.

It was unsustainable, and he'd known that before long it would be noted. And then anxious discussions would be had and the wheels would turn and a smiling face would invite him into an office and nudge him towards the sabbatical he ought to have taken years before.

'It'll give you the opportunity to really concentrate on your research, Richard. Take whatever time you need. Just come back to us refreshed.'

Of course, he knew that they were thinking of themselves rather than him. Shunt him out now and they could avoid all the difficulties and embarrassments that would become manifest when the tidal wave of grief finally crashed on Dr Willoughby and he drowned in the middle of a lecture on Persepolis or Lascaux.

Responsibility for getting him to take some leave had devolved to Stella Wicklow, who had received her doctorate the same year as him but had had a great deal more ambition and risen to head of department.

'Look,' she said. 'Think of them doing Juliette a favour rather than you an injustice. I'm sure she'd appreciate you being at home at the moment, wouldn't she?'

At first that had been true, but not now.

When Richard took off the headphones he could hear Juliette crying softly again in the room above. He was determined to let her after what she'd said.

~

From the scullery he picked up his wellingtons, and from the cupboard under the stairs he collected the butane lantern and the matches, shaking the box to make sure there were some left. Then, dressed in his university scarf and the tweed coat Juliette had bought him one Christmas, he closed the front door behind him and went down the driveway, leaving bootprints a foot deep.

The shooters had gone home with their illicit bags of game, and the living birds had returned to the sky: a curlew softly lamenting, three buzzards banking mutely over the fells. In the wintertime there was often a profound quietness in the dale, especially up here on the edge of the moor. The lane that ran past the house

8

– the top road, as it was known – had no other function than to connect one lonely place with another: Micklebrow with Stythwaite, which sat two miles from the house along the vale, the roofs and chimneys bundled around the church tower.

Across the lane was the field – his field, it was still strange to say – which sloped down to the wood and the beck. This little plot of land was one of the things that had attracted Juliette to Starve Acre in the first place. As far as she was concerned there was no better gift they could give their children than a natural playground that grew as they grew.

On the other side of the valley, beyond the Westburys' hayfield, the limestone terraces of Outrake Fell looked even more severe than usual with their fringes of icicles, and the Burnsalls' sheep, which were normally left to look after themselves on the high pastures during the winter, were down in the farm. The sound of their bleating rose with the slow smoke from the cottage chimney. It was the kind of scene that Juliette had imagined before they'd come to live here. A simplicity of movements and sounds.

Opening the field gate, Richard waded through the snow and headed for the tent that he'd set up before

Christmas. It was a good solid bit of kit, army surplus, and had stayed put during even the wildest weather.

October had been full of cold, brilliant sunshine, but November had brought gales and endless rain. Any ditches Richard dug had been quickly filled with oily green water and so one particularly sodden afternoon he'd driven down to Gordon Lambwell's to see if he had anything useful for sale.

Gordon, who'd been a friend of his parents, lived just outside Stythwaite on the road to Settle – a separation that suited both him and the villagers. His bungalow had the look of a Swiss cottage and behind it lay several acres of scrub and sheds where he kept his goods. Although the side of his van claimed that he dealt in antiques, the word was used in its loosest sense to mean anything that was old, and his outhouses were crammed with junk.

Up in the rafters of a tin-roofed shack he'd found a canvas tent bundled together with its poles and brought it down in a snowfall of dust. Richard had tried to pay him for it, of course, but Gordon had been reluctant to take his money for fear that it would seem as though he were endorsing the project and encouraging Richard to carry on. He was convinced that Richard's father's decline had been caused by him grubbing about in the mud at Starve Acre.

'Are you really sure you ought to be digging there?' he said.

'I can't see that I've much choice,' Richard replied. 'It's the only way I'll know if the roots still exist.'

'Best left undisturbed, if you ask me.'

'If I lived by that maxim, Gordon, I'd be out of a job.'

'All the same, I'd rather you stayed away from that field.'

'Haunted, is it?' said Richard.

Gordon smiled sardonically, changed the subject and took him into the house for a drink. 'And how's Juliette?' he said. 'Tell her that she must come and see me.'

She did.

And that had been the start of her obsession with Mrs Forde and the Beacons.

According to Gordon, the tent had been used in the war, though which war and for what purpose was uncertain. There were stains on the door flaps that looked remarkably like blood. Nevertheless, the material was of a sound, old-fashioned quality, as thick as a sail, and when the rain was blearing across the field Richard was always warm and dry.

After the previous night's dump of snow, the tent had been half buried like many of the farmhouses in the dale. Only the ridge was showing and Richard had to kick the drift apart to get to the entrance. The animal tracks he'd seen from the study window made a detour here and inside the air was ripe with the sweet rankle of fox shit. The vixen that lived in the wood had been back, drawn either by the scent of the tea mug he'd forgotten to take back to the house, or the memory of kindness.

One afternoon a few weeks previously, he'd seen her coming up from the wood, a bright burn of amber in the snow.

When she spied Richard she stopped and stared, her mouth open, giving out white breaths. It was obvious that she was desperate for food like every-thing else, and he went back into the tent for the biscuits he'd brought. At the sound of him rustling the packet, the vixen shied away but soon came forward again, her timidity beaten by hunger. Shivering in her coat, she licked the broken digestives from his hand and allowed him to lay the back of his finger on her snout.

The fox had been the only thing of interest that day and every day that followed. The spade and the trowel had turned up precisely nothing.

Still, he'd known from the start that the whole venture would be something of a lottery. Centuries ago, the field had been part of a much larger common land and so it was difficult to know exactly where the Stythwaite Oak had once stood. As such, Richard's nominal plan had been to start in the centre of the plot and then move in increments as if he were going around a clock face.

If the tree had been as old and vast as the stories suggested then it must have had roots like Yggdrasil. But he had prepared himself for the fact that there might be little or nothing left to find at all. Most of the rainwater swept down the hillside and ended up in the beck and so the field wasn't boggy enough to preserve wood. Yet there was a chance that there might be fragments here and there.

He dug through the snow to find the pegs of the guy-ropes. With these unhitched, he lifted the fly sheet from the poles and laid it down on the drifts. The rectangular ditch of brown soil looked odd among so much white and caught the eyes of the rooks which descended

13

now, peering for grubs and worms. As Richard disman-
tled the frame, more of them settled on the wall, voic-
ing their impatience, hoarsely demanding that he work
somewhere else. But they could poke about here all
day and not find a single thing to eat. The place was
barren.

Taking up the poles, Richard carried them some ten
yards further round the wheel he had envisaged and
reassembled the uprights and the ridge in the place
where he would dig next. With the snow shovelled
away to the bare earth, he set up the rest of the tent,
tautening the ropes, making sure that everything was
weatherproof.

By the end of the process he was sweating under his
coat and yet his toes and hands were numb. The shelter gave only an illusion of warmth, but nevertheless
he was glad to get inside. He lit the gas lamp with a
soft pup and let it burn for a few minutes, rubbing his
palms together, wishing that he'd brought a flask of
tea.

When he could feel his fingertips again, he took out
his notebook and wrote the date at the top of a blank
sheet. Then, having held the pages open with stones
on the square of tarpaulin he used to keep his knees
from getting soaked, he unbuckled the roll of tools.

With pegs and string and a trowel he marked out the six by four rectangle he would excavate, with margins wide enough for him to move around it without having to press his back against the canvas.

Having been insulated by the snow, the ground was claggy rather than frozen and peeled away from the edge of the trowel like curls of hard butter. Progress was, as always, slow and methodical and he dropped each bladeful into a sieve, dicing it up to see if there were anything inside, any indication that he might be close. But there was nothing.

Not that it mattered. Experience had taught him to be patient. Anyway, he was in no hurry to get finished. Away from the house he found a degree of peace. Ewan never bothered him out here in the field.

He worked for an hour and was digging deeper into one of the corners when he felt the trowel scrape across something hard. Using his fingers, he removed the mud more carefully and found the rim of a small pelvic bone.

As he cleared away one patch of soil after another, the rest of the skeleton was revealed. It was of a super-lative delicacy and he willed himself not to break any of it, especially the skull which came out last.

15

It was a cat, he thought – their tortoiseshell, Lolly, who'd run away a year ago – or a rabbit or a fox cub. But then, on closer inspection, he knew it was a hare. Very likely it had been caught by a stray dog from the village or the vixen in the wood. Though when he brought the light closer to the carcass, it seemed too neat to be that of a creature killed by sharp teeth.

For the pelage, skin, muscle and fat to have rotted so cleanly and for the skeleton to be so perfectly preserved the animal had to have died naturally and lain in the field for some time. Richard wondered if he'd come across a collapsed rabbit warren. Not that the hare would have dug out the tunnel itself, but if it had been sick and old then it might well have commandeered some quiet hollow under the ground in which to expire. Either that, or the animal had been interred here deliberately. It was the kind of thing his father might have done in his last manic days at Starve Acre. Perhaps he'd found the hare on the lane and laid it to rest as he'd done with any dead thing he came across: spiders, birds, mice, he'd given them all a proper burial.

However they had come to be here, Richard couldn't leave the remains to be nosed apart by whatever came sniffing around, and so he took off his coat, laid it down and began to pick the bones out of the hole. Each one came away cleanly from its neighbour and in his hands they felt stronger than they looked, robust enough to be carried home.

~

As so few people passed Starve Acre, it was possible to tell from the tenor of an engine who was coming before they appeared. There was a subtle difference between the Drewitts' tractor and the Burnsalls'; between the laboured shudders of the Westburys' cattle truck and the whine and backfire of Gordon Lambwell's Bedford. A stranger could not help but herald their own arrival.

Just before one, Richard heard an unfamiliar car coming up the lane and eventually Juliette's sister, Harrie, approached in her tea-coloured Austin, the headlights bright in the gloom. When she pulled into the driveway, she sat for a few moments regarding the house and the piles of snow. He knew she'd be asking herself the same questions as always. How had Juliette ended up in such a place? Was this really what she wanted?

Having braced herself for the cold air, she got out, buttoned up a long sheepskin coat and lifted her suit-case from the boot. With her other hand, she opened one of the back doors and a little Pekinese dog jumped down on to the icy gravel. She was a haughty creature and, despite being told not to, she cocked her leg and pissed against the tyre. When she had finished, Harrie attached her lead and then yanked her over to the front steps.

Richard waited until Harrie had rung for a third time before letting her in and found her sour-faced and shivering on the porch.

'I was starting to think you weren't actually at home,' she said, staring at his grimy shirt and trousers as she wiped her feet on the mat.

'Didn't hear you, sorry,' said Richard and brought her case inside, placing it by the stairs to take up later.

Juliette had told her not to come, but of course Harrie hadn't taken any notice and so a compromise had been reached. She would stay a few days, a week at the most. But it felt as if she'd brought enough for a month.

'I did say one o'clock,' she said over the sound of the yapping dog. 'Didn't Juliette tell you?'

'I must have lost track of time,' Richard replied.

She didn't believe him, and told him so with a flat look before taking off her scarf.

Under her coat she wore a twin-set the same shade as her car. The blouse was a modest green. Her shoes smugly practical. She had always seemed so much older than Juliette, mostly because she was the veteran of one marriage already – a brief shackling to a wealthy, violent man called Rod who'd put her in hospital more than once. By contrast, marriage number two was happily staid and predictable. She and Graham had three children: wholesome twin boys and a little girl called Shona who was dressed like a doll and given expensive presents that generally turned out to be temporary novelties. She might well have loved and petted Cass, the Pekinese, on Christmas morning but by New Year's Day the animal had probably been sent out to the garden. Now Cass was her mother's responsibility.

She barked again and Harrie picked her up.

'So, how is she today?' she said, resigned already to her sister being no better.

'She's just getting dressed,' said Richard. He found it a pleasure to lie to her.

'At this time? You know she really ought to be up and about much earlier,' Harrie said, closing her eyes as the dog licked the underside of her chin.

'She doesn't sleep well,' said Richard. 'She gets tired.'

'Tired? How can she be tired when she's in bed all day? She's lethargic. There is a difference. When was the last time she went out of the house?'

'Monday,' said Richard. That was also untrue. Juliette hadn't been out for months.

'Well, that's one thing I can do,' said Harrie. 'Make sure she gets plenty of fresh air. I mean, that is why you moved here, isn't it?'

'Look, don't expect too much of her,' Richard said. 'She won't be any different just because you've come.'

'I don't know,' said Harrie, arranging her hair in the mirror. 'It seems to me that if Juliette's going to get better then a change is exactly what she needs.'

'You're not going to talk her out of it,' Richard insisted. 'She's made up her mind about this Mrs Forde coming over.'

Harrie plainly thought otherwise and moved past him to the stairs with the dog under her arm.

'Where are you going?' Richard said.

'She must be dressed by now,' replied Harrie. 'That was what you said, wasn't it? That she was awake and getting dressed?'

'I'll go. Let me bring her down,' said Richard and Harrie stepped aside with a smile, her first skirmish won.

*

20

Outside what had been Ewan's room Richard could hear Juliette's soft breathing. She had evidently cried herself back to sleep and he stepped in quietly.

From a neutral white nursery, the room had become an honouring of all things boyish as Ewan got older. Racing cars circuited the walls in a frieze that Richard had spent a day trying to level and still wasn't quite right. Juliette had decorated the gable end with a cartoon of a smiling dragon and on the ceiling a spiral galaxy spun around the lampshade. The shelves that Richard had built were full of books about castles and knights, tenacious dogs and witless giants. Under the window, next to the rocking chair in which Juliette had fed Ewan the breast and the bottle, a wooden train track lay in an ampersand of curves and bridges with a little red steam engine waiting at the station.

It was all as Ewan had left it. Even his bedsheets hadn't been changed. Richard hated coming in here and often didn't, preferring to communicate with Juliette through the wood of the door, or to leave her alone altogether if she were being as hurtful as she'd been that morning.

Having another child wouldn't be a replacement. He hadn't meant that at all. Of course he missed Ewan.

How could she think that he didn't? What did she want to see? His broken heart on a platter?

But that wasn't what they'd actually been arguing about. Juliette was simply angry that he'd asked the same question again: 'Is this really what you want? For this woman to come?'

'You don't need to say it with such contempt.'

'But is it?'

'More than anything,' she replied.

There'd been an urgency to her voice. Richard knew that she was desperate not to slip back to how she'd been in the first few weeks after Ewan's death. She'd gone about in physical pain. She'd moved from one room to another with uncertainty, as though she were lost in her own home. It had been the same for him too. Each day he felt disorientated and nauseous, oddly disconnected from what was happening in the land of the unbereaved. He found himself shaking for no particular reason. He drank too much and ate too little. He couldn't sit still. His dreams were barbaric.

The new term hadn't come quickly enough.

Months had passed since then, but time felt too insubstantial to be a buffer against a return to those feelings. Still, the problem was his own. This Mrs

Forde and her friends certainly wouldn't provide the solution.

'What if nothing happens when she comes?' he'd said. 'Where will that leave you?'

'You don't have to be there,' she said. 'In fact, I'd rather you kept away, if you're determined to ruin it for me.'

'I've already organised with Gordon to take the test,' Richard told her. 'I'm going to see him tonight.'

Expecting her to be angry with him for making the arrangement behind her back, he'd got in first with, 'I thought you'd be pleased, Juliette.'

'I might have been, if you weren't intent on treating me like a child, Richard.'

'Can't I be concerned for you?'

'I don't want you there just because you think I need protecting.'

'But you know nothing about these people.'

'I know Gordon. I trust him. Don't you?'

'I trust the man, certainly,' Richard answered. 'His ideas, no.'

'Then you stay in your study when they come.'

'I'm not letting you see them on your own.'

She smiled with a quiet assurance. 'Yes, well, I don't think you'll have much choice. You won't pass the test. You're too cynical.'

'What's wrong with wanting some proof?'

'This is proof,' she said, brandishing her notebook at him. 'I'm not mad, Richard, despite what you think.'

The pages were filled with lists of all the moments of contact she'd had with Ewan since the funeral. Lists that had become much shorter in the last few weeks, sending her into an even deeper despondency. Hoping to pick up the faintest traces of Ewan that she believed were still left in his room, she used Richard's portable Sony to make recordings each evening and had filled the place with mirrors. They sat on the window ledge and the chest of drawers, on the bedside table and against the walls, so that wherever Richard looked one reflected another and the room fell away into infinity.

When she was asleep under the covers he could sometimes pretend that there was nothing wrong with her at all. It didn't seem impossible that she might wake up one morning restored, her mind settled by simple rest. Yet rest was hard to come by, not only because her senses were so alert all the time but because of what she slept on. Since Ewan had gone, she'd spent every night here on a mattress she'd dragged up from one of the other bedrooms. She'd kept it from her days at nursing college and the fabric had turned so thread-bare that the spirals of the springs were showing through. It got cold in Ewan's room too and during the night she'd taken the patchwork throw off the rocking chair and added it to the layers of blankets that were pulled tight to her body.

Kneeling down, Richard put his hand on her shoulder. She stirred and blinked at him, recoiling from his touch.

'It's all right,' he said. 'It's just me.'

She glanced around the room, looking, as always, for Ewan.

'Harrie's here,' he said.

'Already?'

'It is one.'

'I can't see her now,' Juliette said. 'Tell her I'm tired.'

He watched the thin muscles in her neck moving under her skin as she rolled away from him. Given all that had happened, it was hardly strange that she'd lost weight but lately he thought that the bone of her clavicle looked even more prominent and her cheeks sharper. If he could hold her body against his, he would no doubt be shocked at how slight she was, but they hadn't shared a bed for months now. It had been his suggestion – if Juliette could only find rest in Ewan's room, then so be it. Yet he lay awake most nights in the hope that she might slip in beside him. She never did. She would only ever wake him if she thought Ewan was in the house.

'Stop staring,' she said, her mouth against the pillow. 'I can feel you looking at me.'

'You'd better get up,' said Richard. 'You know what Harrie's like. She'll only come and fetch you herself.'

'So?' said Juliette. 'Let her. Then I can tell her to piss off in person.'

'You'd say that to her, would you?'

'She's wasting her time,' Juliette said. 'I'm not changing my mind. I've waited too long.'

Richard went down to the kitchen and while he was making tea and listening to Harrie talk about Graham and the children, Juliette appeared in a black turtle-neck and the jeans she wore day in, day out.

Harrie left her cigarette in the ashtray and got up to hug her.

'You look thinner,' she said as the dog who'd been removed from her knee pined for attention.

'What have you brought that thing for?' said Juliette.

Harrie scooped the animal into her arms and sat down again. 'They'd all ignore you at home, wouldn't they?' she said. 'Poor Cass. Aren't you eating, Jules?'

'I'm eating,' said Juliette. 'Don't start.'

'But are you eating enough?' said Harrie, looking her over. 'You're nothing but bones, girl.'

Juliette took a seat on the other side of the table.

'I'm fine,' she said. 'I told you on the phone you didn't need to come.'

'I thought you might want to see your family,' said Harrie. 'Or is that too ridiculous?'

'I can look after myself,' said Juliette.

'It's not just about you. What about Mum and Dad?'

'What about them?'

'You can't keep telling them not to come or ignoring their phone calls. It's unfair. I hate the fact that I've had to keep this secret from them.'

Since Christmas, Juliette had been finding various ways to prevent anyone from visiting. She'd only given in to her sister on the proviso she came to Starve Acre alone.

'All they do is fuss,' said Juliette. 'It's not helpful.'

'But you need people around you, Jules.'

27

'I've got people around me already. People who understand.'

'Aye, so I hear,' said Harrie, picking her cigarette out of the ashtray.

'Meaning?'

'That you're still determined to welcome these head-cases into your house. And I don't know what that look's for. Time was you'd have called them worse than that yourself.'

'Well, I was as ignorant then as you are now.'

'You don't believe in all this crap, do you, Richard?' said Harrie.

'Juliette and I have already had this conversation,' he replied.

'And you're still letting her have them over?'

'Excuse me,' said Juliette. 'He's not letting me do anything. I don't need anyone's permission.'

'Take some advice then,' said Harrie. 'Tell them not to come. This isn't the way to get over what happened to Ewan.'

'And you'd know, would you?'

Richard could see that Harrie was on the verge of losing her temper. She exhaled and clipped the ash off the end of her cigarette.

'Look,' she said. 'It's not just me. Mum and Dad

would say the same. Especially Mum. You know what she's like about this kind of thing.'

'What kind of thing?'

'Ouija boards and table tapping.'

'That's not what the Beacons do,' Juliette replied. 'They're not that kind of group.'

'The Beacons?' said Harrie. 'Jesus.'

'What are you laughing at?' said Juliette. 'You know nothing about it.'

'I know they'll fill your head with all kinds of nonsense,' Harrie said. 'And that's the last thing you need at the moment.'

'And what do I need?'

'To come back to the real world, Jules. You won't get better by locking yourself away.'

'I'm not.'

'Please,' said Harrie. 'I know for a fact you haven't set foot outside that front door since the last time I came to see you.'

Juliette said nothing. Harrie sent the dog away and moved closer.

'Look, no one's insisting that you go back to work tomorrow,' she went on. 'But you do need to get out of this house. Not for long. Just a wee walk somewhere. See how it is.'

'I have been out,' said Juliette.

Harrie shook her head. 'Jules, you know that I've always been able to tell when you're lying.'

The hierarchy reaffirmed, Juliette's belligerence fell away and she looked at her sister as she might have done when they were children. She could only plead for Harrie to understand.

'He's still here in the house, Harriet,' she said. 'I know he is.'

'Oh, Jules, come on,' said Harrie, docking her cigarette. 'Whatever you think you've seen or heard, it's not real. Ewan's dead, love.'

Juliette began to cry and Harrie embraced her, looking at Richard as if to excuse him from the table.

~

He took Harrie's case up to the spare bedroom and then went to the study, hoping to shut himself away and examine the hare's bones more closely. But Harrie being in the house had brought Ewan back to the fore-front of his mind. He could see the boy sitting across the kitchen table from his auntie, staring at the scar Rod had given her. A white, three-inch tick from the time he'd shattered her cheekbone with his heel. Ewan had no idea where the injury had come from but with a child's intuition he seemed to associate it with Harrie's terseness. To him, she carried her unpleasant past with her like a scent and he always kept his distance whenever she visited.

Once, Richard caught him putting the final touches to a portrait of a heavily built woman dressed in brown, her eyes manic, her teeth like a shark's. Richard censured him about it because he had to, really, and told him to keep it under his bed so that Auntie Harriet wouldn't see. Ewan did as he was told but Richard couldn't work out if he was embarrassed, angry or pleased with himself. He had a thousand different expressions. Richard remembered them all. And yet he never once thought that he could read the boy.

Thoughts of Ewan crowded in, rapidly growing large and loud as they'd done that morning. Trying without success to will them away, Richard turned his attention to the shelves instead and searched for the volume on mammal anatomy that he remembered seeing some while ago. Somewhere.

The study was overrun with his father's books. Richard had started trying to catalogue them years before and was still doing so now, in what felt like a

Herculean labour. The mess continued to astound him, not least how quickly it had been achieved.

His father had once taken as much pleasure in organising his library as in absorbing its contents, and he made it his aim to classify his collection to such an extent of specificity that a person could ask to see something on the most obscure of subjects and he would be able to find it instantly. In this little room, he had arranged the physical world, the whole of history, into something as watertight as a policy document. And yet what took him decades to build, he managed to dismantle in less than a week. Before they finally drove him off to Brackenburn he'd removed every single book from its carefully considered position and either burned it in the back garden or packed it away for safekeeping.

His growing sense of despair had worsened to the point of paranoia, and he became fixated on the thought that someone was coming to take his library away; someone who would make nefarious use of the knowledge it contained. '*Mea culpa, mea maxima culpa,*' he'd say, assured that the order upon which he'd insisted would be the world's undoing. With everything categorised so thoroughly, it would be easy for this determined someone to realise their plans. It was for the good of mankind, he said, that everything ought to be either destroyed or hidden. No one had been able to convince him otherwise and by the time the ambulance came, the shelves had been stripped and their contents mixed up in dozens of cardboard boxes.

It would have been perfectly reasonable for someone who hadn't known him to assume that Richard's father had been an academic, but he had never set foot in a university in his life. For thirty years he'd worked in the legal department of an insurance company in Sheffield, ascending from clerk to manager, and it always surprised Richard how much affection folk had for this fussy, private man whose interest lay in things like waterwheels and Tudor shillings rather than people. Whenever he met any of his colleagues, the old guard and juniors alike left an impression of John Willoughby being somewhere between an affable football coach and a fondly remembered NCO. Wilby, they called him.

Considering that he'd fared rather badly at school, he'd advanced beyond most people's expectations and put it down to holding more stock in what he could teach himself than what someone else could tell him.

If he'd had his way, then Richard might have been allowed to learn at home rather than at school. But Richard's mother, recanting on her socialist faith in comprehensive education, sent him first to Bishop Harcourt's and then, after his eleven plus, to Newlands, where he boarded until he was eighteen.

Even in the holidays, Richard rarely 'came home' as such. Summers were spent with cousins in Galway. Christmases at his maternal grandparents' house in Harrogate. Like those places, Starve Acre was somewhere that he visited rather than lived. It belonged exclusively to his parents; it was the stage for their life, not his. Until, that is, his mother died, and he inherited everything.

Juliette had been to Starve Acre a number of times over the years but never once talked about what it might be like to call it home, even though she knew that one day it would be theirs. That she rarely discussed his parents' house at all indicated to Richard that she didn't much care for it. He wasn't surprised. His mother and father had lived almost entirely separate lives within its walls and given the place an air of unhappiness that even the least sensitive visitor found hard to ignore.

Yet, when the chance came to move there, Juliette was certain that they should. She had always hated living in Leeds. For her, the traffic and concrete made for an unpleasantness that found its way into some of the people too. There was always vandalism at the bus station, their neighbour a few doors down had been mugged for his pension money in the subway and every day the *Post* ran stories about violence and cruelty. She saw it herself at work often enough. After the pubs closed, Accident and Emergency was always full. She was convinced that sooner or later the city would touch them in some awful way too.

'Aren't we just trying to have the best life we can, Richard?' she said, when he laughed at her unease. 'Surely we're more likely to find that in the Dales? It must be better to raise children there. Think of all that land we'd have for a start.'

She assumed that through his own experience Richard would agree. But he told her, being away at school, he'd had little interest in the acre of muck or the tangled wood as a child. What lay on the other side of the lane from the house was simply background scenery to him. It was only his father who ever went there, walking the dog, digging for old coins.

'There are plenty of houses,' Richard argued. 'Why does it have to be Starve Acre?'

'Because it came to us,' said Juliette. 'Don't you think we're meant to be there?'

When they drove across a few days after his mother's cremation to try to gather the necessary bits of paperwork for the solicitor, Richard hoped that the foul weather that morning would show the house and its bleak setting in the most honest way and that the romantic fallacies Juliette still harboured about living there would be quickly dispelled.

But once they were out of Leeds, the clouds gave way to wide sunlight that inked the shadows of trees on to the fields and turned the becks in the valleys a glassy blue. In Stythwaite, the main street was busy with people garlanding the lampposts and stringing up bunting for the spring fair. Juliette, he knew, was imagining what it would be like to be engaged in such a happy civic bustle, to be one of the committee members setting out the trestle tables or one of the ladies sweeping the pathway through the graveyard.

Past Cannon's grocery, they skirted the meadow at the edge of the village, the grass already thick and green. April fell through the windscreen and as they made their way up on to the top road Juliette wound down her window, letting the air rush in with the smell of earth and leaves and the flinty noise of the sparrows in the hedges. At the corner by the pines, they came across a gang of children, the Burnsall girls and two little Drewitts leading a pony down to the village, and Juliette turned to Richard as if to say: see? They could be Willoughbys.

Another bend, a steeper rise, and then the lane flattened out and Starve Acre came into sight, its three storeys clad in heavy stone, the windows shuttered, the front door a utilitarian black. Happened upon like this, it was an ugly place, Richard always thought. A place to peer at from a moving car and let dwindle in the rear-view mirror thinking about the poor souls who lived there. On the edge of the moor, it was like a lighthouse, conspicuous and solitary. And now that Richard's mother had gone, it felt as if the very last dregs of life there had dwindled away.

But for Juliette, the sense of absence made the house seem new, and she stood in the hallway taking in the light and space as though she'd never noticed it before.

As they walked from room to room trying to locate bank books and insurance policies, gas bills and mortgage statements, Richard could tell that Juliette was tempering her plans with discretion. His mother had only just been laid to rest and she didn't want to seem mercenary. But it was clear that she was already filling the house with their furniture and their tastes and their children.

She worked on him gently but persistently in the weeks that followed and such was her certainty about transferring their lives to Starve Acre that Richard couldn't help visualising what their future might actually look like in that stack of high-ceilinged rooms. He found that if he thought of it in that way, as just a house and not his parents' former home, then it didn't seem quite so strange a proposition for them to go and live there.

He pictured the front room. A winter's night. A fire. Outside, silence: miles of it. He pictured the kitchen with its Belfast sink and its wooden racks and pulleys, and saw a dozen of their friends gathered around the table laughing and arguing as Juliette carved a joint of meat. Up on the first floor, he saw himself typing in what had been his father's study, and the three bedrooms opposite waiting to be filled with little Willoughbys. At the top of the house, the room that his parents had used for storage became, in this vision, the place where he and Juliette slept together. Across the landing was the nursery, where he found a wooden crib and watched their first child, a son, sleeping under a blanket, his chest rising and falling, his hands clamped into pudgy little fists on either side of his head.

~

They moved at the start of August, when Juliette had finally been allowed some leave from the infirmary, and settled in before the demands of the new term became too overwhelming for Richard. Ever the logistician, Juliette suggested that they concentrate on one room at a time, and days were spent systematically removing Richard's parents' things and shoving and swearing their own furniture into place. When they got hungry, they'd cook. When they didn't have the strength to lift anything else or the inclination to unpack another box, they went to bed and enjoyed one another drowsily in the top of their tower before falling asleep. Then, the next morning, Juliette would be awake early stripping off the old wallpaper or fitting a new light bulb or sitting cross-legged in front of the range trying to understand the mysteries of its flues and valves.

It was infectious to be with someone who was so sure about what they wanted. To Juliette, problems were welcome, because solving them was a means of dispensing with the old and replacing with the new. Any difficulties that arose were just waymarkers on the route to making Starve Acre their own. But she was never so swept up in it all that she became impatient. She was prepared for the fact that the place would only become theirs incrementally.

Even so, their possessions took up so little space that the house felt larger and colder to Richard than it ever had. Their sofa was lost in the front room. Their plates and bowls all fitted into one cupboard. They hadn't enough photographs to line the width of a window ledge and even with all their paintings hung, the rooms still sounded cavernous, especially the kitchen, where the clock seemed to mark the passing time twice. It was hard not to think of himself as an intruder here; a feeling that was strongest whenever he went into the study, and it became clear that if he was ever going to consider Starve Acre his home, then he would have to face the mounds of clutter that his father had left.

He had no appetite to remake the library in its former image, but he felt that there should be some order to it, if only to see clearly what was there. And so, if he ever had a spare hour he would work on 'Magna Congestus' (as it became known) and pick up from where he'd left off, opening another box and sorting through the books. It was a tedious process, but it meant that he came across some things that he didn't know his father had owned, like the woodblock prints of the Stythwaite Oak.

It was purely by chance that he found them, pressed inside a heavy volume on the Mongol empire. They were small, early seventeenth century, he thought, by the composition. Probably pre-Civil War. Originals, too, from the look of the paper. The work was nothing to rival Holbein or Dürer, but far better than average. Any crudeness in the cutting was due to the poor quality of the material into which the designs had been carved rather than a lack of skill in the craftsman. Without the luxury of sanded boxwood in this part of the world, he'd undoubtably used sections from the dead oak tree itself, and it was possible to see where his burin had slipped and followed the warp of the grain.

The edges of the prints were either torn or perforated with needle holes, meaning that they had probably come from a larger collection, and Richard suspected that the whole had been reduced to its parts during his father's demented reshuffling and that there were more sheets loose in the study somewhere.

The four scenes he had found so far corresponded to the four seasons and were a sort of overture of the tree's changing shape and communal usage during the year.

In *Springe* a young couple courted under the budding branches. In *Merrie Maye* children danced in a ring around the trunk and then in *Autumn* they were back, collecting acorns and firewood.

In the last picture, where the tree was a maze of bare branches, a man climbed up· a ladder to the bough labelled Olde Juſtice with a noose in his hand.

Richard looked out of the window at the white rolling of the dale. He would have given anything to have seen the Stythwaite Oak on a wintry evening like this; the shadow of its great cranium of branches splayed across the snow, a centuries-old behemoth that had – so they said – seen sixteen kings and queens from Plantagenets to Stuarts come and go. If all that were true and if it had lived longer, then it might have become as well known as the Selborne Yew or the Tolpuddle Sycamore, but no record of it survived apart from the woodblock prints and a handful of stories that naturally contradicted one another. The only point of agreement was that the tree had died unexpectedly. In which case it seemed obvious to Richard that it had suffered from some kind of fungal infestation, or had even been struck by lightning. That at least would have given weight to Gordon's yarn about the tree's ruin being a punishment for putting one of God's creations to such brutal purpose.

'You do know they used the tree for hangings, don't you, Richard?'

'Yes, Gordon.'

'That's the reason nothing grows there in your field.'

'Yes, Gordon.'

'There's not an inch of soil that's still alive.'

Local lore had it that the divine reprisal had not ended with the tree but had spread out across the common in a poisonous ripple, turning the grass black, seeping down into the earth like oil, suffocating the life out of the place.

Time had inevitably fattened the myths about Starve Acre, and yet it was undeniably sterile – most noticeably in the summertime, when all along the dale the fields belonging to the Burnsalls and Drewitts and

Westburys were verdant and the Willoughbys' plot was nothing but dry mud.

In all the digging he'd done, Richard had never once turned up a single worm or spider. Only bones.

His coat was still on the desk where he'd left it, the arms folded and the hood and hem tucked in. When he opened it up, the hare's carcass was a jumble, but the book of anatomical diagrams he'd been looking for would help him reassemble the pieces. He found it eventually between a biography of Nicolas Flamel and Plutarch's *Isis and Osiris*. It was a battered volume, the stitching loose and the cover nubbed at the corners. But the drawings of the various skeletons had been kept pristine by sheets of tissue paper and between gull, black-headed and harrier, hen he came to hare, common.

Under the desk lamp, he cleaned the bones with cotton buds and warm water, finding that beneath the dirt they were not the stained, mouldering brown he'd expected of things pulled from the soil but looked bleached, as if by a desert sun.

He picked out the skull and held it in his palm. Its weight was barely noticeable, like an egg shell or a ball of paper. It was a beautiful object. The brain cavity was intricately terraced and sutured, the mesh of the nasal passages woven out of hair-thin filaments of bone. Both sets of incisors were still intact, white and sharp as splinters of chalk, and the molars were solidly fixed in the jaw. What dominated his attention, though, was the eye sockets. They seemed too wide and too deep, as though this were the skull of a large bird.

With a pair of tweezers, he began to sort through the individual vertebrae, arranging them inside a cardboard box in order of shape and size. Piece by piece he rebuilt the hare just as it appeared in the book, just as he had found it in the field. Though laid out here in the study it looked so much bigger.

From the base of the skull, the bones arched and thickened through the lumbar region before narrowing towards the tail which curved like the crack-end of a whip. The shoulder blades were sharp and translucent. The ribs made a strong coop. But it was the hind legs that fascinated him most – the way that speed and spring still seemed ready to burst from the joints. In life, it would have been a magnificent animal. Ewan would have been captivated by it.

~

He would often come into the study while Richard was working. He'd steal in, actually, and ten minutes might pass before the boy made his presence known. Then, dressed as a wizard or a fireman or a prince he'd sit quietly on Richard's knee and leaf through picture books; or he'd ask to feed a sheet of paper into the typewriter and jab the keys, fascinated by the noise and magic of the mechanisms. This was Ewan, not what other people said of him. He wasn't vicious or cruel. There were reasons for what had happened at school with Susan Drewitt. Richard hoped that everyone might see that now and think of Ewan with sympathy given that he had passed away, but judgements about people tended to become fixed in the village for considerable lengths of time.

Richard had learned from his father long ago that Stythwaite opinion was worthless. Certainly not something that one should expend any energy in opposing. Left alone and unnourished by concern, it would have to feed on itself like an ouroboros and eventually die. Well, it had been easy for his father to say that; he hadn't sent his son to the village school and could be as indifferent as he liked about what folk thought of him. Besides, he'd retired to the dale to get away from people, to put several miles between himself and his nearest neighbours. It was Richard's mother who'd done her best to ingratiate herself with those in the village.

When they lived in Sheffield she'd been chairwoman of a poor relief committee that sought to alleviate the suffering of those bombed out of their homes by the Luftwaffe. It was a role that kept her busy for some time and it was almost ten years after the war ended that she and Richard's father finally moved to Croftendale. She found no less hardship there either. Though the scale of want was naturally smaller here in the countryside, her proletarian brothers and sisters still felt the bite of deprivation, especially the elderly. Every other day she'd cycle down from Starve Acre to visit lonely widows or gouty, wheezing gentlemen inva- lided out of some back-breaking rural industry. She'd cook, she'd clean, she'd write their shopping lists and at the weekends she'd drive the Ford Anglia to Cannon's and collect the groceries she thought they needed most.

One such Saturday, as his mother was driving back out of Stythwaite, the Somertons' dog had got loose and, having been shooed out of the churchyard, it careered across the road and under the wheels of the car. Hearing the noise, the villagers poured out of their

47

cottages and the afternoon drinkers from the pub. The priest phoned the policeman in Lastingly and the whole village kept Richard's mother there on the street until the constable arrived. The Somertons, in particular, had been insistent that she was charged with something, but the policeman didn't need much encouragement to give Mrs Willoughby notice to present herself at the station in Skipton on Monday with her documents. Then came the line that she'd taken to heart for years afterwards.

'I don't know how you drive in town, love, but you slow down when you come through here,' he said. 'It might not be a dog next time. It might be a little lad. You wouldn't want some idiot knocking the life out of your child, would you? You think about that when you get behind the wheel.'

What a thing to say. Couldn't he see that she was pregnant?

'Skipton, first thing Monday,' he said, and then finding no one willing to remove the dog from under the car he took hold of its back legs and dragged it to the kerb.

All this had happened in the mysterious world that preceded Richard's birth, where the roots of his parents' unfathomable habits and decisions lay. As he grew up, the story about the Somertons' dog had explained a few of their foibles but it still left the most important questions unanswered. The mongrel had been one of a dozen that mooched about the village. Had his mother really been so ashamed of killing it that she couldn't face anyone in Stythwaite ever again? Had there been so much hostility towards the Willoughbys that Richard had been sent to a boarding school miles away? It seemed unlikely. Yet, as a child, it was difficult to know what to think.

No one had ever talked to him about the incident, of course. Even Audrey Cannon, the expert rumour-monger of the grocery shop, was still tight-lipped when it came to Edith Willoughby. She meant well, love, was all she'd ever given away.

She meant well. Meaning: she'd tried too hard. Meaning: that her benevolence had been taken as interference. They hadn't wanted her smiles or her cups of tea or her home-made cakes. They hadn't wanted her attention or an ear to bend. Nor a walk around the village or another chapter of *The Ragged Trousered Philanthropists* or *Jude the Obscure*.

Richard imagined that they tolerated her at first, the way they might have waited out a storm, but then they'd have started talking – in the King's Head or after mass, where he pictured her altruism being broken and shared like another round of communion bread. Their collective indignation had nothing to do with a dead dog. His mother had simply embarrassed them all. It hadn't occurred to the villagers that they either needed charity or that they ought to show it to each other.

He told Juliette very little about any of this. Like his mother, she had come here to live with others, not as an outcast. And while it was obvious that she'd have a hard time being accepted as an equal, Richard gave her whatever encouragement she needed to join the Fair Committee or the PTA. They were civil to her, rather than friendly, though Juliette seemed to think that that would change over time if they could see that she was serious about being a part of the village.

But after what Ewan had done to Susan Drewitt at school, he was afraid that all the effort she'd made would come to nothing and that people would think of the Willoughbys as they'd always thought of them.

It had angered him more than he imagined it would and he suspected that some of that sentiment came across in the meeting with Ewan's teacher. It wasn't a denial of the facts as they stood – Ewan had hurt the girl on purpose, and had admitted to holding her fingers in the jamb of the closing door – it was the situation. A cloud would be cast over Juliette's belief (and therefore his own) that they'd made the right decision in moving here, and the boy would be tarnished with a reputation he didn't need.

Although, at the time, Juliette hadn't been thinking of notoriety. She just wanted to understand why Ewan had done it. He had never been violent before. Not once. He was a boy of simple pleasures. All that summer before he started school, he'd been content just to look for birds in the back garden or fly his kite on the moor. On other days, he'd explore the field, digging like Daddy did, trying to find treasure. There'd been no sign that he would turn in such a sudden way.

His attack on the Drewitts' girl being so random, so out of character, made it all the harder for Juliette to take. She blamed herself. The lessons she thought she'd taught him about friendship and kindness had obviously been inadequate.

But, as Richard explained to her, Ewan had only been at Holy Cross a few weeks when it happened: perhaps he'd merely taken out his anxieties about starting school on someone else. It had to be said, too, that Miss Clarke was young and inexperienced, insensitive as yet to the nuances of children's behaviour, too broad in her brushstrokes. She'd painted Ewan as the aggressor and Susan as the innocent victim, but who knew, really, whether either of those labels was entirely accurate?

And perhaps a veteran teacher might have seen that it was only pent-up frustration boiling over. Ewan had always been a little behind the others. Not quite as quick to count numbers, or recognise letters, never quite clapping to the beat. But, as everyone liked to reassure Richard and Juliette with great authority, he was only that way because he'd been born early. He'd soon catch up. There would be plenty of time. Children had it in such abundance that they could throw it away and waste it just as they pleased. For them, it would simply unfold and unfold. Only, it hadn't. Not for Ewan.

~

Richard worked in the study until dusk fell. Harrie ran Juliette a bath and then went to the kitchen to cook. A while later, when the water was draining away, Richard heard her calling.

'Jules, there's food on the table when you're dressed,' she said.

'I don't want anything,' Juliette replied.

'Well, sit down with us anyway.'

'I told you,' said Juliette, coming out of the bathroom now. 'I'm not hungry.'

'You must be. Come and have something at least.'

'It's nearly seven,' Juliette said, and Richard listened to her going up to the top floor.

'Hold on, I'm talking to you,' said Harrie. 'Don't you go back to that bloody room.'

She followed Juliette, calling her back, demanding that she eat, but Richard knew that she was wasting her breath. Seven o'clock had been Ewan's bedtime and since his passing it was the moment of the day when Juliette most felt his presence. Nothing would keep her from being in his room when the clock struck the hour.

Realising that her orders were being ignored, Harrie softened her tone.

'Why don't you sleep with me tonight?' she said. 'You could bring the mattress and put it next to my bed, like you used to do.'

'We're not children, Harriet,' Juliette replied.

'It'll give us a chance to talk.'

'I don't want to talk.'

'It doesn't have to be about Ewan. We can talk about anything. I've not seen you for months.'

Juliette responded by firmly closing the door to Ewan's room and Harrie spent another few minutes knocking and negotiating with her until she finally gave up and came back downstairs. Richard couldn't help but feel a degree of satisfaction at her defeat. It was just like her to think that she'd be able to walk into the house and change everything with a clap of her hands. And if she couldn't, then she'd assume that it was only because Juliette was being deliberately obtuse.

'I mean, does she actually want to get better?' she said, quizzing Richard as he put on his coat and scarf in the hallway. 'I just don't understand why she's being so resistant. What is it she wants?'

'You're asking the wrong person,' he said, glad that he had the excuse to leave and go to Gordon's.

~

The wipers carved off thick wedges of snow from the windscreen and Richard crunched out of the driveway, following Teddy Burnsall as he cleared the lane.

Although the worst that the weather had thrown down was sheared aside by the blade of the tractor's plough, there were still patches of ice where the wheels of the car would spin before they gained the traction of the tarmac again.

Richard came to the village tense and jittery and was grateful to see the church tower at last. The doors were open and the lights were on. It was the night the bell ringers practised. The last of them, late and hurrying, waved to Teddy as he swung around the corner by the edge of the graveyard and headed towards his farm. Everyone in the village seemed to consider him a decent man and had been outraged on his behalf after what Ewan had done to his horse at the spring fair the year before.

But the boy had been goaded and that always exacerbated his difficulties. The Burnsalls' daughters had to take some responsibility.

Over the bridge, Richard passed along the main road – the curtains in the cottages all drawn, the windows of the King's Head steamed up – and out beyond the last streetlight to Gordon's place, which in the dark always seemed much further away.

When the headlights caught the faces of the stone lions, Richard turned between the gateposts and followed the cracked driveway to the house. As soon as he pulled up, two St Bernards appeared and kept him in the car until Gordon came to the front door and sent them lumbering around the corner.

'Aren't dogs vile?' he said, as Richard made his way up the steps. 'I'd shoot the pair of them if it were up to me. If you get a move on, the tea shouldn't be too stewed.'

He left Richard stamping the snow off his shoes and called from the front room.

'Felicitations, it's still drinkable. And, Richard, don't let that fucking cat in. She's being an unalloyed madam at the moment. I've told her the furniture's Arts and Crafts, but she just looks at me and carries on scratching.'

The ash-blue Persian in the hallway scrutinised Richard and darted away into the junk-filled recesses of the house before she could be picked up.

Every time Richard visited Gordon it was more noticeable that the domestic function of each room was rapidly becoming overtaken by the commercial. Things that he hoped to sell were heaped every-where. The front room had too many clocks, too many radios, too many televisions, too many paintings. It reminded Richard of the Royal Academy exhibitions where the pictures were stacked from floor to ceiling.

Gordon offered him one of the unmatching chairs by the gas fire, briskly sweeping the velvet cushion free of cat hairs.

'Sorry,' he said. 'I've told Russell to trim the damned thing, but he won't, of course. Not after last time. She turns into a perfect devil if you try to hold her down. Between you, me and the four walls, I'm just waiting for the opportunity to drown the little fucker in the bathtub. There.'

Replacing the cushion, he patted the seat and smiled. As he'd got older he'd become fleshier in the nose and lips, and had started to take on more than a passing resemblance to Dylan Thomas. He dressed like him too in a bow tie and a three-piece suit pungent with an aftershave that smelled of cloves.

He took hold of Richard's hands as he sat down and turned them over. The lines on his palms had gone black with soil.

'You're still digging then?' he said.

'I'm still digging and I'm still alive.'

Gordon frowned at his flippancy. 'Has anything turned up?'

'Not yet,' said Richard, thinking better of telling him about the hare's skeleton.

'You've been prowling about in that place for months,' said Gordon. 'And you've found nothing? I don't believe it.'

'It's not that unusual, I can tell you.'

Gordon poured the tea. 'At what stage do you decide that the whole thing's otiose and call it a day?' he said. 'Or are you going to take up the entire field?'

'Don't you think the roots are there?' asked Richard.

'I think there's something there,' said Gordon. 'Yes, you may well smile, but I've lived here longer than you and I've seen things.'

'Seen things?'

'In the mind's eye, yes.'

'Like what?'

Gordon considered the question. 'Things left over,' he said.

'How do you mean?'

'It's hard to put my finger on it exactly. But you certainly couldn't make me go through that gate. Your father could never persuade me to go burrowing with him.'

'He was only after old pennies, Gordon.'

'What you go searching for and what you find aren't always the same.'

'Did you get that from a Christmas cracker?'

'I'm not talking proverbially, smart arse. I'm talking from experience. I don't like the place.'

Seeing Richard's reaction, he laughed, though without much humour.

'Your father used to give me that look,' he said. 'He thought I was barking too. They all do, don't they, apart from you, sparrow?'

He directed this at Russell, who came in with the cat in his arms. He was a pale, demure lad with thick copper curls and, at nineteen or twenty, was one of the younger lodgers Gordon had taken in over the years. He sat down on the arm of Gordon's chair, trying not to let Richard see that he had a black eye. Turning away a little more, he allowed the cat to rub her cheek against his hand.

'I don't know what you see in that animal,' said Gordon.

'Companionship mostly,' Russell replied. It was clearly a pointed remark, but Gordon didn't react.

'Well,' he said, 'you tell your friend that next time she gets at the furniture I'll pluck those claws out. Or get Richard to bury her in the field.'

The smile he passed over with the cup of tea was difficult to read. It was often hard to gauge him, actually. That was part of his charm and it was one of the reasons they didn't much care for him in Stythwaite. But then unless one had family pedigrees that stretched back so far as to be forgotten, they didn't really care for anyone much.

Gordon was an outsider, just as Richard's mother had become. It had made them natural allies. Ewan, too, had picked up on the fact that Gordon was somehow separate from the folk in the village, and they had bonded with a surprising devotion. Whenever they were together, Richard and Juliette watched Ewan transform into an animated, gregarious boy they barely recognised. He'd adored Gordon and Gordon had been exceptionally protective over him. He fussed about so many things when it came to Ewan that Richard and Juliette thought that his concerns could only really be an affectation. He must have known that they weren't about to let Ewan hurt himself in all the ways he feared. They'd hardly let him drown in the beck or fall out of a tree. And they couldn't see what harm would come to him across the lane. In any case, they'd moved to Starve Acre so that Ewan could enjoy the outdoors and Gordon knew that.

Yet he always seemed determined to direct Ewan's attention away from the field. He'd brought him a record player and provided his first bicycle. He'd drive up to the house with books he'd picked up from the second-hand fairs and read to him. That was what Ewan looked forward to the most, even if the stories were always a little too mature for him to fully understand. It was the way Gordon told them that he enjoyed. Even Juliette sat and listened. People did when Gordon spoke. Especially at the memorial service, when he'd recited so passionately the text of Corinthians 15.

In those vague, blank weeks that followed the funeral, Richard and Juliette had spent more time with him than they had when Ewan was alive, the three of them propping each other up at the worst moments. Juliette, especially, found Gordon a great comfort; he was attentive to her when Richard was at work. But what seemed obvious now was that he had been weighing her up and waiting for the right time to tell her about Mrs Forde and the Beacons.

Still, he'd been led by his heart. Richard had to remember that. He had been lost once, just as they were.

A number of years before, another of his lodgers – it was Gordon's euphemism – had been killed in an accident on the motorway and Mrs Forde had been the one to lead him out of the maze of his grief.

That he'd been wary of her at first was something he'd confided in Richard many times in order to persuade him that his feelings about her would change too.

'I was just as doubtful as you are,' he'd say. 'I was quite convinced that she wouldn't have any answers. And she didn't.'

Then he'd lean in, *sotto voce*.

'I did, Richard.'

She had not given him counsel, it seemed, but simply made him notice what he already knew, what he intuitively felt about the afterlife. It was, he said, so simple that he laughed when he realised how easily it had been overlooked. This sudden seeing had had such a profound effect on him that he'd aided Mrs Forde with her ministrations ever since, driving her all over the county so that she could attend to the bereaved. Richard had no doubt that Gordon just wanted others to benefit from the insight he'd been given but it seemed as though he were trying to find some way to repay her too. She refused to take any money in return for what she did and, though Gordon thought it honourable, it made Richard all the more concerned. It would have been better if she had asked Juliette to cross her palm with silver; at least then her motivations would be transparent. He'd rather she was a business-woman plain and simple than someone so convinced of their numinous gifts that they felt it a duty to share them out of charity.

Outside, the two dogs barked at a passing car. Russell fidgeted anxiously and left the cat with Gordon.

'I'll go and get things ready,' he said.

'Yes, go on, sparrow. You fly off,' said Gordon.

'What happened to his eye?' said Richard when he'd gone.

'He was shopping for me at Cannon's and fell foul of some bastards coming out of the pub,' said Gordon. 'He won't say who, but I have my suspicions. That's why the dogs roam freely. They're for his sake rather than mine. I've long since given up being afraid of the rebarbative little shits around here.'

'You get it everywhere, Gordon.'

'Yes, but I think we have a rather inimitable species of cretin in Stythwaite. I've not forgotten the way they treated your mother.'

'That was a long time ago.'

'Or what they thought of Ewan.'

'I don't care about that any more.'

Gordon saw straight through him – he always could – and changed tack.

'How are things at the house?' he said. 'How's Juliette?'

'Her sister's arrived.'

He smiled in his knowing way. 'You seem put out, Richard,' he said. 'I'd have thought an ally would be welcome.'

'Harrie doesn't understand enough about it.'

'Nonetheless, I'm sure she wants what you want,' said Gordon.

'Which is?'

'To persuade us not to come.'

'And is that possible?'

'It was Juliette's decision to start this process,' said Gordon. 'It must be her decision to stop it too. You can appreciate that, Richard, I'm sure. You can't choose for her.'

'Even if she can't see the harm she's doing to herself?' Richard replied.

Gordon looked genuinely perplexed. 'What harm would happiness do to her?'

'It's the disappointment I'm worried about,' said Richard.

'There won't be any disappointment. Mrs Forde hasn't failed anyone yet.'

'Well, that's what she would say.'

'Richard, I can assure you she's not a mountebank.'

'Fine, fine,' said Richard. 'I'd rather we just got it over and done with.'

'And have the whole farce exposed, eh?' said Gordon.

He smiled and put his cup down on the saucer.

'You know, I don't think you're entirely cynical, Richard,' he said. 'Otherwise you wouldn't be so upset with me.'

'Sorry?'

'Well, if you truly believed that there wasn't anything after all this,' he said, looking around the room, 'then it wouldn't matter what I or Mrs Forde or anyone else said to the contrary, would it?'

'So?'

'So, don't be so dismissive, Richard. You might be surprised. An open mind can only help you move forward.'

'I am moving forward.'

'I hope that's true,' said Gordon.

It still chastened Richard that Gordon had seen him at his worst in the days after the burial. He'd watched him get resolutely drunk, astonishingly drunk, in this very room. He'd watched him holding his head as though it might split wide open from the swell of thoughts. The images of Ewan and his laughter and the thousand recollected dialogues were brutally invasive even when he was soused on Gordon's home-made gin. It was only when he finally fell into the void of sleep that he found peace, although it was a peace that he was not conscious of enjoying and when he woke again the assault immediately resumed.

'Ewan's dead,' said Richard. 'Being open-minded isn't going to change that.'

'I know he is,' Gordon replied. 'I'm not saying that we can bring him back.'

'Well, that's what Juliette seems to be expecting.'

'It's not uncommon for people to misunderstand what we do.'

'I just don't want Juliette hurt by false promises,' said Richard. 'That's all.'

'Is that all? Or are you worried that we'll let something wicked into your house? I told you, Richard,' said Gordon with a laugh in his voice, 'it's not a fucking séance.'

'I know it's not.'

'Mrs Forde doesn't make the lampshades rattle.'

'I didn't think she did.'

'Then what are you so anxious about? The test?'

'Not really. If Juliette passed, shouldn't I?'

'Richard, I've already forewarned you that there's no guarantee of that.'

'But I'm not letting Juliette go through the sitting on her own.'

'No, no of course,' said Gordon. 'Look, drink your tea and then we'll go into the bathroom. It won't take long. Russell's quick. Medical student.'

'I know.'

Russell's choice of career was a source of great pride for Gordon and he took every opportunity to mention it.

Richard drained what was left in his cup and followed him down to the damp, tiled cubby-hole next to the kitchen, where Russell was washing his hands.

'Will you be coming too?' Richard said, then wondered if it were improper to ask someone outright if they were a Beacon.

Gordon answered for him. 'No, unfortunately

67

Russell didn't pass,' he said. 'Mind you, I wasn't particularly surprised. You were ruined by a revolting Catholic childhood, weren't you, sparrow? It's left him entirely adverse to the concept of a soul, poor lad.'

Russell patted his skin dry with a towel and glanced at Richard.

'Roll up your sleeve,' he said.

From the mirrored cabinet, he took down a plastic box and indicated for Richard to sit on the edge of the bath.

'I'll keep it in the fridge until Peter comes to collect it in the morning,' said Gordon. 'It's better cold, apparently.'

'Peter?'

'Mrs Forde's assistant.'

'And what exactly does she look for?' said Richard, turning back his cuff.

'I really couldn't tell you. She just knows it when she sees it, I suppose. You've not had a drink, have you?'

'Not for a few days, no.'

'Good,' said Gordon. 'It can scupper the reading.'

Russell had been waiting for them to stop talking and when Gordon nodded he peeled off the lid of the box and took out a syringe.

~

Snow was falling again when Richard left, his arm throbbing dully under the dressing that Russell had taped to his skin.

Driving along the street, he found himself behind Father Moston as he cut through the slush on a bicycle. Closer to the church, the priest lifted one leg over the crossbar and balanced on the pedal until he came to a stop by the lych-gate.

Pale and gangly as an adolescent, he had the plain appearance of a man who was required to shape his face into an assortment of expressions. He did 'compassion' and 'consolation' well and had made the funeral service more or less endurable on that August afternoon too beautiful for a burial. He'd said all the right things and read from the Gospel of John with what had seemed to be a genuine feeling of hope.

This is indeed the will of my Father, that all who see the Son and believe in him may have eternal life; and I will raise them up on the last day.

The will of Richard's father had been to ensure that his son was in no doubt that a church was merely a meeting place for the mentally ill, and that all who gathered there – priest and parishioners – were as fearful and asinine as schizophrenics. There was no God, no devil, no heaven or hell, no posthumous judgement for wickedness or reward for piety; there was no resurrection, no transfiguration, no illimitable bliss, no life everlasting. The sum of human existence was collagen and calcium phosphate. And then nothing.

For several years now, Richard had initiated his undergraduates with a slideshow of photographs he'd taken on the research trips he'd made before Ewan was born. He gave them no warning of what they were about to see. That was the point. Their reaction was the lesson.

Here were the bones of St Hyacinth in Fürstenfeld. St Erasmus's astonished skull in Munich. Here was the crypt in Palermo and the dozens of mummified priests, each still dressed in his robes and biretta, each noseless face dry and mottled like the rind of a strong cheese.

Look at the Catholic Incorruptibles, he'd say, still sweetly perfumed and pliable after hundreds of years. Imelda Lambertini, Anna Maria Taigi, the beautiful Bernadette Soubirous.

He'd ask the class if they found themselves fascinated or repulsed as he sent around photographs of the Bolivian *ñatitas* – the decorated skulls and infant skeletons that shared houses with the living. Wasn't it more respectful to do this than consign the dear departed to a box or a bonfire? he'd say. Wouldn't one wish to have some physical presence after death?

He played devil's advocate, but always privately sided with those students who could see the love that rested in these relics.

Now, since Ewan had gone, he thought that there was a great decency in oblivion.

There was no point in preserving the boy's belongings like the artefacts of a museum. Everything – every last toy and every piece of clothing – ought to be thrown into the stream of time to float away. The murals on his walls ought to be whitewashed and the windows cleaned and the room filled with the noise of a new child. Not to forget Ewan, but only to acknowledge that he wasn't coming back.

~

In the small hours, Richard woke to hear Harrie calling for Juliette downstairs. He found her standing at the front door, wrapped in her coat and wearing a hat that she'd taken from the stand in the hallway. In her arms, the dog yipped and shivered.

'What's wrong?' said Richard. 'Why are you up?'

'She's out in the bloody field,' said Harrie and, looking across the lane, Richard saw the ray from a torch spiking over the snow.

He went out, following the holes that Juliette had made, realising quickly that he had too few clothes on. A sharp wind was coming down the valley, bending the trees that Juliette was prodding with the light.

'Juliette? What are you doing?' he said and was answered by a bright stare from her torch.

'Have you seen him?' she said. She was holding one of Ewan's teddy bears by its neck.

'It's three in the morning. Come inside.'

'But I heard him,' said Juliette. 'And look.'

She took Richard's sleeve and pulled him over to a bank of snow near the gate. 'Those tracks,' she said.

'A fox,' said Richard. Probably the vixen that he'd fed a few weeks before.

But Juliette had already walked away to investigate a different part of the field.

'Surely you heard him too?' she said. 'He was laughing so loud he woke me up.'

'You were dreaming then.'

'I wasn't dreaming. I know the difference,' Juliette replied, lighting up the house and catching Harrie's anxious face.

Something that Richard couldn't see attracted her attention and she made her way through the thick drifts towards the wood.

'Ewan?' she called. 'I'm here.'

She swung the light through the trunks.

'There. There, didn't you see him?'

'Come back inside now,' said Richard. 'It feels like it's going to snow.'

But Juliette tramped further between the trees and shouted for Ewan again, her voice carrying little further than the torch beam before it was swallowed by the night.

It was only when the wind raised a blizzard that Juliette returned, crying and clay-cold. Harrie took her into the kitchen, where she relit the woodstove and wrapped her in a blanket. The corners of the windows filled up quickly with snow.

The storm had not been forecast at all and stripped the ash trees of whatever deadwood was still clinging on. It wouldn't have been a surprise if the power were to suddenly cut out. It often happened in the dale.

On one such occasion in the November of Ewan's first term at school – when the lines had been snapped by a fallen tree along the lane – Richard and Juliette woke to the smell of burning. It was coming from outside their room and when they stepped on to the landing, trying the light switches, smoke was seeping out under Ewan's door.

Richard went in and found the metal waste bin on fire and Ewan sitting cross-legged in the glow.

'Good God, what are you doing?' Juliette said and snatched him out of harm's way as Richard used the beaker of water by the bed to put out the flames. The pile of old colouring books and comics collapsed and ash billowed up into his face.

As Juliette carried Ewan out of the room, he kicked and screamed and beat his fists against her back until Richard managed to disentangle him.

'Stop it, Ewan,' he said. 'You're hurting Mummy.'

But the boy seemed not to care and Richard pulled him hard by the wrist into the dark of the master bedroom, causing him to howl and fight even more. So much so that Richard had to hold him in a bear hug for a full minute before he calmed down.

The lights came back on and Juliette, who'd been standing irresolutely in the doorway, sat Ewan on the bed and cradled him against her.

*

Breathless from the effort of restraining the boy, Richard leaned against the dressing table.

'What were you thinking?' he said. 'You could have set the whole house on fire.'

Ewan wouldn't look at him.

Juliette tried instead. 'Why did you do it, love?' she asked. 'You must have known it was dangerous.'

'I didn't like the dark,' said Ewan.

'The dark's nothing to be frightened of,' said Juliette. 'We've told you that.'

'But it was talking to me,' Ewan said.

Juliette looked at Richard.

'Where did you get the matches from?' he said. 'From the kitchen? From the box by the fireplace? Under the stairs?'

'Didn't use matches,' said Ewan.

'What then?' Juliette asked.

'Daddy's sparker,' said Ewan, and mimed with his thumb.

'Did you go into the study?' Richard said and Ewan dipped his head.

Juliette looked at Richard reproachfully and then asked Ewan what he'd done with the lighter.

He took it out of the pocket of his dressing gown and handed it over. Richard was surprised that it had still been there in the drawer of the desk. He hadn't smoked for years.

'In,' said Juliette and peeled back the blanket.

The boy complied and lay there, small and tearful, while Juliette settled herself beside him. She seemed to sense Richard's resentment at being ousted.

'Well, he can't stay in his own room tonight, can he?' she said. 'You find somewhere else to sleep.'

The next day they'd taken Ewan to see Dr Ellis in the village. The boy had been coughing all night and Juliette was worried about his lungs. Coming into the world six weeks ahead of time, he'd never been a strong child.

Ellis looked into Ewan's mouth and then lifted his sweater and pressed the end of the stethoscope to his back.

'All clear,' he said. 'His throat's a bit sore, but it'll be better in a day or two, I'm sure. Just give him plenty of water to drink.'

Ewan slid down off the trolley-bed and Ellis ruffled his hair. He was a tall, broad man, headmasterly but avuncular, and used to the company of children. On his desk was a photograph of his sons and daughters.

Four altogether. The amount Richard and Juliette had planned. It had seemed to them the right number. In a trio, there'd always be somebody left out and five felt like one too many. With four, there could be parity.

'Water, all right,' said Juliette. 'Thank you.'

'Could have been worse,' said Ellis.

'Yes,' Juliette replied, helping Ewan put on his coat.

The look she gave the boy as she tugged hard at the zip suggested that he hadn't yet been forgiven.

Ellis caught her expression too and he called for the nurse to take Ewan outside.

'Why don't you go and choose a lollipop, young man?' he said. 'I hear that they're excellent for sore throats.'

Ewan went out holding the nurse's hand and Ellis closed the door.

'I take it the fire wasn't accidental?' he said.

Juliette shook her head and explained what had happened.

'You know,' said Ellis, once she'd finished, 'there's a small part of me that admires his resourcefulness. But as you say, it was somewhat dangerous.'

'He must have known that,' said Juliette. 'I mean we've told him and told him not to play around with fire.'

'In my experience repetition isn't always a guarantee of obedience,' said Ellis.

'I know,' said Juliette. 'But Ewan's not stupid. He must have been aware of what might happen.'

'He is only five,' said Richard.

'Which is why you should have kept the study locked,' Juliette threw back.

Ellis sat down and smiled at them both to keep the peace.

'Children experiment,' he said. 'I'm not sure there's much you can do to stop it short of caging them up. In fact, that's probably the worst thing you can do for a lad like Ewan.'

'Like Ewan?' said Juliette. 'What do you mean?'

Ellis knew that he had chosen his words badly and apologised by lifting his hands off the desk.

'Someone who clearly enjoys being outdoors was what I meant,' he said.

Juliette sat forward. 'So we shouldn't be worried about him?'

'Are you?' said Ellis.

'I don't know,' said Juliette. 'He just seems so different now he's at school.'

'Wouldn't you say that was inevitable?' said Ellis, looking from her to Richard. 'It would be more unusual if he'd stayed the same.'

'Of course,' Richard replied.

'But to be so changed?' said Juliette. 'To be this vindictive.'

'Vindictive?' Ellis said.

'Come on, I can't imagine that you haven't heard about what happened with Susan Drewitt by now,' said Juliette. 'It must have been you who strapped up her fingers.'

Caught out, Ellis said, 'You're certain that Ewan meant to do it?'

'He said so,' Richard replied.

'You don't think he's . . .?' said Juliette, trying to find and avoid the word at the same time.

'No, I don't,' said Ellis. 'He's a perfectly normal, healthy boy. And you both know that too.'

Juliette thought about it. 'But he just wants to spend so much time alone.'

'Some children do,' said Ellis. 'My eldest is still happier in her own company.'

'But he isn't happy,' Juliette said. 'He's lonely.'

'He'll patch things up with his classmates soon enough,' said Ellis. 'Children don't tend to live in the past as much as we do. Anyway,' he went on, getting up when he heard the nurse's voice. 'It's not so long until Christmas. I'm sure that'll be a good diversion for him, won't it?'

The nurse knocked and brought Ewan in with the bulb of a lollipop swelling his cheek.

He'd said nothing all the way back home but stared out of the car window, licking sugar syrup off his fingers. When they pulled into the driveway, he looked warily out of the rear window at the field. The night before had been so wild that the boy had probably mistaken the sound of the thrashing trees for the voices in his room. Richard suggested that he go across the lane, if only so that he knew there was nothing there to be afraid of.

'Go on,' he said. 'While it's not raining.'

With some hesitancy, Ewan got out and went to the edge of the road. He looked both ways as they'd taught him and then squeezed between the gate and the post.

'You're happy to just let him go off and play, are you?' said Juliette. 'After what's happened?'

'I'll keep an eye on him from the study,' Richard said. 'He'll be fine.'

But that wasn't what she meant.

'Don't you think there ought to be some consequences for what he did?' she said.

Richard's feeling was that he'd learned his lesson

already. Seeing his parents angry and upset with him was punishment enough.

Juliette watched the boy capering his way through the field, his night terrors evaporated by daylight. 'Well, I don't see any remorse in him,' she said.

'And what would remorse look like in a five-year-old exactly?' said Richard. 'He's forgotten about it. So should we.'

'It's not that easy.'

'Try.'

Juliette conceded for the moment and went into the house to start cleaning Ewan's room.

As he sat at his desk and typed, Richard watched the boy gathering up the debris from the storm. He began to make a pile of dead wood in the middle of the field, and what looked alarmingly like a bonfire at first turned out to be a sort of castle. The construction kept him busy for some time and became interwoven with a game in which the large branch he straddled was transformed into a majestic horse. There was no point expecting him to be contrite. If anyone ought to feel guilty, thought Richard, then it was him and Juliette, not Ewan. It shouldn't have been so easy for him to find the lighter and put himself in danger. But not only that, it was the assumptions they'd held about him that were making all this seem so much worse than it was. He'd always been such an obedient lad that Richard wouldn't have imagined he'd even think about going into the study if he'd been told not to, let alone rummage through the drawers. He'd acted out of character, but it was a character that they had moulded for him. Ellis had been right: children changed.

He'd been right, too, about Ewan needing space to play. Over in the field, the boy was immersed in his own world as he rode to and from the fringes of the wood gathering twigs with yellow leaves to act as flags for his battlements.

Each journey seemed to be rife with danger, as he veered around enemies and swashed the air with a stick sword. The route he took from his castle to the wood was the same each time and so while this episode of the game persisted, Richard could put him in the peripheries of his sight as he worked, knowing that he would not stray far. It was only when the motion of the little figure suddenly stopped that Richard turned his attention fully to the window.

Ewan was standing very still by the pile of branches he'd made, gazing up into the sky. Richard followed

his line of sight, but he couldn't see any birds or aero-
planes – the kinds of things that the boy often pointed
out.

Still staring, Ewan dropped the foliage he was carrying, backed away and then ran up the field towards the
house.

~

The snowstorm lasted for most of the night, and in the
morning Harrie let Juliette sleep until ten before going
up to her room with some tea. She spoke softly to her
now and tried to coax her down to the kitchen so that
she could cut her hair, though Richard could tell
that she had some ulterior motive.

'You needn't look so worried, Jules,' she said, laying
sheets of newspaper on the floor. 'I always made a
good job of it, didn't I?'

She stood behind Juliette with a brush and drew it
through her hair, making her wince when it caught the
tangles.

'I thought we might go out today,' she said.

'Go out where?' said Richard.

'Down to the village,' Harrie replied, picking up the
scissors from the table. 'You could do with some
groceries.'

'I can't,' said Juliette. 'I need to clean for when Mrs Forde comes. She said that I had to.'

'Well, we don't even have to go as far as the village if you don't want to,' said Harrie. 'We could just walk to the wood or something.'

She made the first cut, sending a sheaf of auburn hair to the floor.

'Didn't you hear me?' said Juliette. 'I have to prepare the house for the Beacons.'

Harrie combed her hair straight again and blew the strays off the scissors.

Coming to the point now, she said, 'Look, there's someone I'd like you to speak to.'

'What are you talking about?' said Juliette. 'Who?'

'He was so good for me after everything that happened with Rod,' said Harrie. 'He's one of those people who make you feel very at ease. I could tell him anything. His name's Osman.'

'Oh, for Christ's sake,' said Juliette, understanding now. 'I'm not seeing your fucking psychiatrist, Harriet. Is that the reason you're here, to drum up some trade for him?'

'You need to talk to someone, Jules.'

'What is it with you and talking? Is that the cure for everything?'

Harrie put down the scissors. 'Listen, it wasn't until Osman got me to open up about Rod that I came anywhere close to moving on. He really straightened me out.'

'I'll bet he did,' said Juliette. 'Does Graham know?'

'I'll put that remark down to your condition.'

'My condition?' said Juliette, getting up. 'What is it you've diagnosed me with exactly?'

'Jules, I've spoken to Osman about this Mrs Forde and he agrees with me that it'd be much better if she didn't come.'

Juliette struggled for words, as she often did when her sister infuriated her, and her response was jumbled.

'Why would I care what this Osman thinks? You had no right . . . he knows nothing about me . . . Jesus, Harriet.'

'Can't you at least hear what he has to say?' said Harrie, directing this to Richard as much as Juliette.

'She doesn't need a psychiatrist,' he said.

'And I already know what he'll say,' said Juliette. 'They're full of it, people in that profession. They send people mad.'

'You're basing that on one experience, Jules.'

'One was enough.'

Ewan had come away from the children's clinic in Wakefield hysterical.

'They don't know what they're talking about half the time,' said Juliette.

'If you think it's all nonsense, then it won't do you any harm to see him, will it?' Harrie retorted.

'Do you think I'm losing it?' said Juliette. 'Is that it?'

'I don't think you're well,' said Harrie. 'Given what you say about Ewan.'

'Why can't it be true? I wouldn't be the first person it's happened to.'

Harrie sighed irritably. 'Oh, listen to yourself. Listen to what you're saying, Jules, for heaven's sake. You can't believe it, surely?'

Juliette left the room and Harrie called after her.

'Your hair. It's not finished.'

When Juliette ignored her, she turned to Richard.

'What are you looking at me like that for?' she said.

'Can't you just let her work things out on her own?'

'Richard, if there's one thing that's clear it's that she's no idea what's best for herself any more. She needs Osman, not these others. Not this Mrs Forde.'

'She's not a vase,' said Richard. 'You can't just tip one thing out and pour another thing in.'

Harrie frowned at him and gave a little exasperated laugh. 'You really can't see how ill she is, can you?'

'Grief isn't an illness.'

'But she isn't grieving. How can she be when she thinks Ewan's alive? She needs help.'

'And you're the remedy?'

'I am on your side, believe it or not.'

'So what do you suggest?'

'That she gets away from this house as soon as possible,' said Harrie. 'And I'm not being dramatic. The longer she stays here the worse she'll get.'

'Where should I take her, exactly?' said Richard. 'This is her home.'

'Let her stay in Edinburgh with me for a while. Give her some time with her family and she'll be a different person the next time you see her. I know she will.'

'Is this why you came?' Richard said. 'To spirit her away?'

'You think she's better off here?' said Harrie, leading him to the door of the kitchen. 'Look at her.'

Juliette was out in the hallway polishing the mirror and listening to the tapes she'd made in Ewan's room. She had the volume dial at its limit and the sound of her own breathing, the rattle of the pipework, the draught from the window and all the other restless

87

movements of the house that she'd recorded were amplified to a deafening cacophony.

~

Harrie tried her best to persuade Juliette out of the house, but she continued to swab and scrub, moving from the hallway to the stairs, where she swept each riser in turn and cleaned the brass rods with a duster.

She hadn't inspected the house so closely since the days following the fire in Ewan's room. Her process had been as meticulous then as it was now. Once she'd got rid of the smell of smoke and taken down the curtains to be washed, she made Richard lock the study and keep it locked whenever he wasn't using it. All the matches were kept in cupboards well out of Ewan's reach and anything else that the boy could conceivably appropriate for mischief was consigned to the shed in the back garden.

Juliette knew perfectly well that it would be impossible to second-guess all the ways in which Ewan might hurt himself, but she felt that she had to do something nonetheless. With the winter approaching, the boy was spending less time in the field and more time in the house. But it didn't seem to Richard that it was anything to do with the weather. The afternoon he'd been out there playing knights and castles after his visit to Dr Ellis he'd come back in troubled by something. And each time he'd been out since he'd only gone as far as the gate before running home.

'What's wrong?' Richard asked him. 'Don't you enjoy going there any more?'

Ewan shrugged and Richard wondered if he'd simply run out of games to play.

'No,' said Ewan. 'I know lots of games.'

'What is it then?'

'I don't like the tree,' Ewan said.

'The trees in the wood, you mean?'

'No, the big tree.'

Now Richard knew why the boy had been staring up into the sky. He'd been picturing the old oak. No doubt Gordon had filled his head with stories.

'But there is no tree in the field,' said Richard. 'Not any more.'

'It's there sometimes,' said Ewan, the logic completely sound to him. 'Sometimes it's not.'

Richard had taken him and shown him that the acre was empty and, holding his hand, Ewan seemed content. But he still wouldn't go there on his own. Instead, when he wasn't at school, he drifted around the house from one room to the next or sat glumly on the stairs dressed as a pirate or a cowboy for a game that had quickly become dull.

Anxious that boredom would lead to curiosity and curiosity to injury, Juliette tried to keep him occupied as much as she could by playing board games or helping him bake biscuits or distracting him with a book or a comic. On Sundays, she and Richard might take him for a walk across the moors towards Micklebrow or drive over to Skipton to look at the castle.

Once, they had gone to stay with Juliette's parents in Edinburgh for the weekend, a tense couple of days during which Eileen and Doug tried to guess why they'd come. Nothing had been said to them about what Ewan had done to Susan Drewitt or about the fire, but they could tell that something was wrong. Juliette spent most of the time fretting over Ewan, whose moods had been impossible to keep up with. He'd been morose and then hyperactive, wanting company one minute and to be alone the next.

'We all need our own space,' Doug had said to comfort Juliette. 'Even at that age. Give him some room to breathe, pet.'

When they got back to Starve Acre, she tried, but each time Ewan went to play in his bedroom Juliette would contrive some reason to go and see him a few minutes later. She'd take up clean clothes or choose that moment to start clearing out his wardrobe or changing his bedding.

In turn, Ewan began to do the same to her.

After putting him to bed and getting into the bath, she might surface from the water to find him watching from the doorway. Or he seemed to have a knack for knowing when Richard and Juliette were in the early stages of foreplay and would get into bed with them before it went any further.

Under the sheets, he'd pinch their skin or pull Juliette's hair, simply because it hurt, it seemed.

'It's all for attention,' Richard said. 'Nothing else.'

'But he doesn't want our attention,' said Juliette. 'He wants to be on his own.'

'Deep down, I mean.'

As far as Richard could see, Ewan was as needful of his parents as any other child.

'Do you like him?' Juliette asked. 'As a person, I mean.'

'Of course,' said Richard. 'Why? Don't you?'

'I don't know,' she said. 'Genuinely. I can't say.'

'He's still our Ewan,' said Richard, and she looked at him as though that were the problem. He was whatever they had made him. If they didn't like what they saw, then it was their own fault.

It seemed to Richard sometimes that Juliette had actually brought twins into the world: Ewan and Guilt. The latter had always been the stronger of the two. It fed more, weighed more, demanded more of their attention. When it had outlived Ewan, it had grown larger still.

Even before she fell pregnant, Juliette had talked about her boy, her Ewan, describing in detail the personality he would have and the clothes he'd wear. And while Richard always thought it nothing more than a rather sweet exercise of the imagination, it shocked other people that Juliette could have so much confidence in an untested womb. They dressed their concerns as jokes but still, the feeling among friends and family had been that Juliette was in danger of jinxing herself and the child in some way, if a child came at all. When she was pregnant, it was easy to dismiss it all as superstition, but then Ewan had been born early and when they tried for a second baby a year later nothing happened. Then the thought that she had been presumptuous and had inflicted some damage on herself was hard to shake off. When Ewan passed away, she was convinced that it had been her who'd invited death to the house.

But whether it had been a punishment or simply harsh biological fate, it didn't much matter in the end. No conclusion seemed to make sense. No one could explain what Ewan's life was supposed to have meant. He'd gone before he could really become anything or achieve anything or make anything. It seemed that he'd only come into the world to take all their love and then fill them with sorrow.

As Juliette swept the landing outside the study, Richard tried to type up the notes he'd made in the tent. But he found himself distracted by the hare and took off the newspaper he'd laid down on top of it to examine the bones again. Quite what he should do with them, he didn't know. To keep them in a box felt like a waste. He could, of course, take the remains to the university when he returned there. Biological Science might want them. Or he could mount the skeleton in some way so that the hare would look as though it were springing across his desk.

He searched the shelves for a book that might explain such a procedure but found nothing of use and resumed the work of unpacking another of his father's boxes.

An hour passed. He sorted what he could into subject groups and added the rest to the ever growing piles of miscellany under the window.

At the bottom of one box, he found a set of books fattened by old envelopes full of dried wildflowers from the garden. And in the middle of a pamphlet on the fly agaric was another of the woodblock prints.

Compared with the others, it was in poor condition. The edges were crumpled and at some point it had been folded into a quarto. The creases had made the paper fragile and so the whole thing came out in four sections that Richard arranged on the desk.

It appeared to show three farmers. One with a cudgel. One with a net. The last, holding a lantern on a pole, knelt in his field saying, 'Jack Grey, Our Bonnie Sonnes Dyed For Thee.'

Richard hadn't heard that name since his childhood, when the Cannon boys in the village shop would try to scare him.

You know Jack Grey lives in the wood by your field, don't you, Willoughby? You know that he comes out at night and looks through your windows?

The older people in Stythwaite had their stories too, about being followed through Croften Wood as children, about their grandfathers warning them to look out for Jack Grey. Though what he would have done to them if he'd caught them creeping through the trees was never clear. And while the thought of being watched as he slept was unsettling, Richard couldn't ever quite picture what he would have seen if he had woken up. Jack Grey was one of those figures who, for some reason, persisted from one generation to the next, becoming ever more obscure until only the name survived, attended by a vague sense of malevolence.

There were comparisons to be made with the kinds of deities that cropped up all over England. He was really just another Green Man or Robin Goodfellow or Hag o' the Hay. The fickle entity that either spoiled or swelled the crop. The whistler in the woods. The stranger on the lane at dusk. Friendly enough, but not entirely trustworthy. A tune on the pipes and then a blade at your throat.

He would have been an ancient thing of folklore even when these prints were being made. It was hard to imagine that anyone had honestly thought him real.

~

Just after six on Sunday evening, Gordon arrived with the Beacons. He came to the door first while the others were getting out of his van. As he shook Richard's hand and kissed Juliette on the cheeks, he seemed unusually on edge.

'Sorry we didn't get here any sooner,' he said, 'but the lane's like an ice rink and the van's not as light on its feet as it was.'

'It's only a few minutes,' said Juliette. 'Don't worry.'

'I know, but Mrs Forde likes to get to people on time,' said Gordon. 'It's important to her.'

He adjusted his tie and looked back at the three people approaching. He was wearing his best suit, Richard noticed.

'Has she told you?' said Juliette.

'About what?' Gordon said.

'About Richard. About whether he can be with us.'

But before Gordon could answer, the others were there at the door and he introduced the well-dressed young man helping Mrs Forde up the steps.

'This is Peter,' he said, and there were firm handshakes.

He looked to Richard like one of the clerks who had worked in his father's office. Every line of him clean and sharp, including the white stripe of scalp in his side parting.

Next to him was a petite middle-aged woman in a mackintosh.

'Rashmi,' she said. She had the yellowish teeth of a heavy smoker. A great abundance of black hair. When she took Richard's hand her wrist rattled with beads.

'And Juliette, Richard,' said Gordon, as Peter and Rashmi unbuttoned their coats, 'this is Mrs Forde.'

Richard had been expecting someone more obviously peculiar but under the gabardine she wore a cotton skirt and a simple ivory-coloured blouse. If he'd passed her in the street he'd have thought her a primary school teacher or a vicar's wife. A plain but attractive woman in her early sixties who clipped her hair in place with a metal butterfly.

In her presence, Gordon was unusually quiet and deferential. And Peter and Rashmi waited on her like the maids of a dowager, taking her jacket and her scarf, picking off stray hairs from her shoulder.

'You have a beautiful house,' she said, her voice kind but brisk.

'Thank you,' said Juliette. 'I cleaned, like you said.'

Mrs Forde looked around approvingly. 'I could tell as soon as I walked in that this is a home you love.

I should think your boy was very happy here, wasn't he?'

Juliette nodded.

'No, no more tears,' said Mrs Forde, passing on the handkerchief that Peter took from his breast pocket. 'I'm sure you've cried enough for him these last few months, haven't you? Make this the last time.'

'I'll try,' said Juliette, smiling as she wiped the corners of her eyes.

'Ewan went very suddenly,' said Gordon, as if to mitigate Juliette's reaction. 'You remember me telling you?'

'I do, I do,' said Mrs Forde. 'Though there is some comfort in knowing that if the light leaves a child, then so much of the suffering of later life is avoided. You'll be familiar with the poem by Jonson, I'm sure?'

'Yes,' said Juliette.

One of the Aberdeen uncles had copied part of it into a sympathy card. 'To have so soon 'scap'd world's and flesh's rage' under a picture of Jesus receiving a dove on to his palm.

After Ewan's death, almost every piece of correspondence that came through the letterbox carried the same assurances that the boy was in heaven and looking down upon them as an angel.

The gist was often no different to those mawkish Victorian pamphlets that testified to heartbroken parents that all suffering was ordained. That no death was chance. That a child was always hand-picked to be with God. It was hard, Richard thought, for people to accept that an event could be utterly devoid of goodness. No one wanted to admit that cruelty really existed. Which is why the letters that came to Starve Acre from second cousins and old school-friends insisted that the experience of Ewan's death would send the Willoughbys out into the rest of their lives with the sort of inner strength that was only ever forged in grief. Meaning that they were privileged in some abhorrent way.

Eventually, Richard stopped looking at the post. Of course, people had to say something, but their presumption to know exactly what he or Juliette were feeling only made him indignant. No one could possibly have understood what they didn't understand themselves. Although Harrie, naturally, claimed otherwise. She always thought she knew best when it came to her sister.

For the last few hours she'd been trying to get Juliette to cancel the Beacons' visit and, having failed, she nodded perfunctorily when they were introduced to her.

Mrs Forde seemed to sense that her contempt was really concern and put her hand on Harrie's shoulder.

'You know, your sister will be quite safe,' she said and Harrie gave a short, incredulous laugh before turning to Juliette.

'If you need me,' she said. 'I'll be in my room.'

'If I need you?' replied Juliette. 'For what?'

'Just take care,' said Harrie and she shifted past the visitors to get to the stairs.

'I'm sorry,' said Juliette, opening the kitchen door for Mrs Forde.

'Don't apologise,' she said. 'I've come across it all my life. You know, for every person like yourself, there are a thousand others who'd rather walk around in ignorance. Still, I understand that in a way it must be comforting to do so for a while.'

'The truth frightens some people,' said Peter, and Rashmi concurred.

'Or they just need proof,' Gordon added.

Richard thought that this was probably directed at him, a hint of the verdict Mrs Forde had reached. It was exactly as he thought: the taking of blood, the play of divination, was just a way of weeding out the sceptics who might show her up as a fraud.

Mrs Forde sat down at the table and smoothed her skirt over her knees.

'What's worrying you, Juliette?' she said. 'You're tense.'

Juliette couldn't really say why and Mrs Forde invited her to sit.

'It won't hurt you, what we do tonight,' she said. 'It won't be frightening. If you feel changed afterwards, then it will only be in a good way. It'll only be like coming out of water and opening your eyes.'

'But will Ewan come back?' asked Juliette, causing Mrs Forde to frown. 'I still don't really understand why I can't see him or hear him any more. Why has he been fading away?'

'I think you've just explained to yourself why you're confused. Ewan Willoughby was just a body. A body can't come back once it's been put in the ground, can it?'

'The light was just passing through him,' said Peter, opening the large leather bag he carried.

'But going where?' said Juliette.

'Ah,' said Mrs Forde. 'Did you ever blow dandelion clocks when you were young?'

The metaphor lost on her, Juliette looked to Gordon.

'The light has a tendency to wander when it's released from the body,' he said, sounding unconvinced that his explanation was any clearer.

101

Rashmi picked up the thread as she gathered her hair into a headscarf, her bangles clacking. 'It's not conscious as such,' she said. 'It doesn't choose what it illuminates next. It can get lost, so to speak. It can drift.'

'But there are some people,' said Mrs Forde, 'like myself, Peter, Gordon and Rashmi – like you too, Juliette – who can draw the light back to where it once flourished, where it gave life to something precious and loved. You can invite it into a new form.'

Juliette caught the noise Richard made and glared at him across the table.

'And what about Richard?' she said. 'Will he be joining us?'

Mrs Forde looked at him, put her hand on his and gave him a benevolent smile. No, thought Richard, he would be banished to the garden like an unwanted dog.

'Of course he can stay,' said Mrs Forde. 'The reading was very strong, very positive.'

Juliette gave Richard an accusatory look, as if he had somehow fixed it to be there. But he was more surprised than her. Surely Gordon had told Mrs Forde how dubious he was about all this. She could have easily ostracised him with her ridiculous haemomancy, but she hadn't.

102

'Shall we begin?' said Mrs Forde.

Peter and Rashmi arranged two large jars on the table. Inside one was a mound of grubby melted wax, inside the other a brand-new white candle. Tipping the first jar, Peter lit the wick and watched it catch and flare. On the table, the shadow of the sooty glass lengthened and shrank and then stretched again as the flame wavered. Gordon rolled down the blinds and switched off the lights.

'Are you ready, Juliette? Richard?' said Mrs Forde and resettled herself in her chair, her hands palm-up on the table.

Peter, Gordon and Rashmi did the same and Juliette copied, encouraging Richard to do likewise.

'Be unshaded,' said Mrs Forde. 'Burn brightly.'

Gordon breathed in and out. 'Burn brightly,' he said.

'Burn brightly,' echoed Peter and Rashmi.

They all held hands and a circle formed.

'Think of the candle flame,' Mrs Forde said to Richard and Juliette. 'Keep that image in your mind and the light that was in Ewan will come back to you.'

Juliette smiled and gripped Gordon's hand tighter.

For five minutes, ten, fifteen (Richard could not help but keep glancing at the clock) they all closed their eyes and breathed slowly, their chests eventually rising and falling in unison.

After some time, the candle burned low and beyond the island of the table the room was entirely dark. Opposite him, Richard watched Juliette shifting in her chair, trying to keep her eyes closed.

'What's wrong?' said Mrs Forde.

'Nothing, nothing,' Juliette said.

'You're distracted. What is it?'

Juliette opened her eyes, causing Mrs Forde to do the same.

'He's standing behind me,' she said. 'I can feel him.'

Mrs Forde held her hand firmly. 'You have to let these illusions go. You have to see that there is only light now, not Ewan.'

'But there he is,' said Juliette, tracking whatever she thought she could see around the room and looking over Peter's shoulder.

'Close your eyes again,' said Mrs Forde. 'Think of the flame, like I said.'

Juliette began to cry. 'I'm sorry, Ewan. Mummy's so sorry.'

'Look at me,' Mrs Forde whispered sharply.

Slowly, Juliette took her eyes away from the dark space and did as Mrs Forde told her.

'This has to end, Juliette. Otherwise you'll be thinking in circles for the rest of your life.'

'But I don't want him to go.'

'He's already gone. He left you six months ago.'

'Don't say that,' Juliette cried.

'But it's true. The only place where Ewan Willoughby still lives is in your mind.'

Juliette sniffed back tears and Gordon kissed her hand.

'She is right,' he said. 'You know she is.'

Rashmi smiled, her eyes still closed, and said, 'You mustn't worry about him, Juliette. All his pain has gone.'

'Where did he like to play?' said Mrs Forde. 'Where was his favourite place?'

'His room,' said Juliette.

'No, no. Somewhere else. Not in the house. What about the field?'

Juliette rejected the idea. 'He didn't always like going there. It frightened him sometimes.'

'He can't be frightened any more,' said Mrs Forde. 'That isn't possible.'

She smoothed Juliette's hair off her brow.

'Can you still see him now?'

'Yes,' said Juliette. 'I think so.'

'Then tell him he can go. Tell him he can go into the field for as long as he likes.'

Juliette did so, her eyes red with tears.

'Don't cry over a thought,' said Mrs Forde. 'That's all your boy has been since he died. Don't fool yourself any more. Close your eyes. Think about the light.'

Juliette steeled herself and wiped her face, though she was still looking at the door.

Once they were all settled again and breathing deeply, Mrs Forde began to repeat a whispered mantra, the words of which Richard couldn't make out but which sounded suitably abstruse. Rashmi, Gordon and Peter joined in too and against the hard walls of the kitchen the sibilance echoed and tangled, the sound now close to Richard's ear, now scuttling around in the beams of the ceiling.

The noise grew into a mesh of voices and counter-voices and Richard felt Mrs Forde's hand tightening on his. Soon, a smile spread across her face and the others grinned too. Peter began to laugh quietly and then Gordon responded. Mrs Forde caught it next, followed by Rashmi then Juliette. Whatever one person saw or felt quickly passed around the circuit.

'Do you see it?'

'Yes, I see it.'

'Yes.'

'Yes.'

But it all skipped Richard and he sensed nothing but the sweatiness of Peter's hand and Mrs Forde's wedding ring digging into his palm.

'It's beautiful.'

'Beautiful.'

'Wonderful.'

'Wonderful.'

'Come in, come in,' Gordon said.

Half enchanted, half alarmed, Juliette said, 'Will it stay?'

'Yes, look, look,' said Mrs Forde.

They all opened their eyes and watched the flame in the jar shiver and distend until it went out in scrolls of grey smoke. The darkness in the room fell in on them. Richard felt hands pressing on his as they all waited.

A few seconds later the new candle sprang into life.

When the flame was still and strong, Mrs Forde broke the circle and Peter passed her a handkerchief to wipe her brow.

'Leave the candle to burn,' she said. 'Don't blow it out. Let it diminish on its own.'

Juliette looked baffled, as if she were coming around from a dose of anaesthetic. Even when the others were hugging one another (and Richard) in a loud chatter of excitement and relief, she said nothing but sat at the table gazing around the room.

'Give her a moment,' said Mrs Forde when Richard went over to speak to her. 'Come into the hall.'

'She'll be all right,' said Gordon as Richard followed him out of the kitchen. 'It's perfectly normal. Some people are like that the first time they see properly.'

'Normal?' said Richard.

But Gordon was unruffled. 'Whatever you think, Richard,' he said. 'You'll find Juliette much happier from now on.'

'You won't recognise her,' said Rashmi, presumably thinking that this would be a positive outcome.

'If she seems strange,' said Peter as he unhooked Mrs Forde's coat from the rack. 'It's only because you've never seen a person really at peace.'

He held the gabardine ready for Mrs Forde to put on, but she walked away from him to the foot of the stairs and looked up into the dark.

'What is it?' said Gordon.

She gripped the banister and went up a few steps, craning her neck to peer at the railings on the landing.

'Mrs Forde? Are you all right?' Rashmi said, trying to work out what she was seeing.

When she came back down, her legs seemed weak and Peter passed her coat to Richard so that he could hold her up.

She had begun to sweat more profusely and Gordon quickly moved the stool from under the telephone table for her to sit on.

'No, no,' she said, turning away from the stairs. 'I'd rather we just left.'

Peter found a fresh handkerchief in his inside pocket and dabbed at her face. Every bit of her skin had a film of moisture and there were dark patches seeping through her clothes.

'Please,' said Mrs Forde, moving Peter's hand away from her. 'Could we go? I need some air.'

Richard gave the coat back to Peter who hung it on Mrs Forde's shoulders before taking her arm.

As she passed him, Richard could see that her lips had turned pale and she had the grey cheeks of some-one about to be sick. Rashmi got the door and held it wide open, gripping Mrs Forde's elbow to help her down the steps.

'I'm sorry, Richard,' said Gordon. 'She does get like this sometimes. It can take it out of her. Tell Juliette I'll come and see her in a day or so, all right?'

Outside, as she waited for Gordon to open the van, Mrs Forde looked over the face of the house and was still staring as they left.

It was an effective piece of drama, Richard thought, for her to leave them in no doubt of her mysticism.

~

In the kitchen, Juliette was transfixed by the candle. As Richard sat next to her, she gave a wry smile, as though in that moment she had realised something that had been eluding her.

'Juliette?' said Richard. 'Are you all right?'

She turned, blinking, not really there.

'What did you see?' he asked.

'Hmm?'

'You said it was beautiful. What was it?'

'It's hard to explain,' Juliette said.

'What were you all laughing about? What was so funny?'

'The absurdity.'

'Of what?'

'Of this,' Juliette said, touching her body.

Harrie came down the stairs and a moment later she edged into the kitchen smoking a cigarette, the little dog following.

'They've gone then?' she said, taking the place that Mrs Forde had occupied and looking suspiciously at the two candles. 'What did they say?'

Juliette didn't respond, but watched the light playing over her hands.

'What's the matter with her?' said Harrie.

'I don't know,' Richard said. 'She won't say.'

'What do you mean, you don't know? You were there, weren't you?'

'I think she just needs some time to herself.'

'Is she drunk?' said Harrie. 'Is that what they did, get her drunk? Jules? Did they give you something?'

She moved closer to Juliette, shaking her arm, trying to rouse her from her bliss.

Richard left them in the kitchen and went up to the study. It had been just as he'd imagined it: nothing more than a grandiose parlour trick. A cut above the fishing wire puppets and phosphorous oils of the Victorian spiritualists, but theatre nonetheless.

Especially Mrs Forde's sudden onset of nausea. The only reason Juliette couldn't see the smoke and mirrors was because she didn't want to.

And they would be back. He knew that. Juliette's state of rapture wouldn't last and then she'd call the Beacons here again. She would become reliant on their performances.

New snow was falling outside, dusting the tent, restarting the process of burial. It might have been the first day of winter, Richard thought, not a few days shy of March.

He wanted thrushes and cuckoos and the green woodpecker in his blood-red bonnet. He wanted catkins, bluebells, brimstones, helleborines. He wanted to see hares on the run, hares on the hunt for does, drunk with the scent of them.

That was how his hare ought to be, not as bones in a box.

Yet, when he removed the sheet of newspaper from the skeleton he could see straight away that some alteration had taken place.

The vertebrae were now connected by little pads of cartilage and the finest webs of sinew held each bone in place.

He tried to recall if some of the joints had been coupled in this way when he'd lifted the remains from the field but he was certain that he would have noticed.

In the drawer, he found the tweezers he'd used when he'd first assembled the skeleton and, gripping one of the shin bones, he pulled gently until the leg was extended. The knee held firm and the ball at the top of the femur was locked tight in the cup of the pelvis.

The candle that the Beacons had left burned through the night and was still alight the following morning. And as Juliette went about with a beatific smile and Harrie tried to wheedle out of her what had happened, the hare continued to change.

When Richard looked inside the box he found that as well as the leg joints being connected, now each piece of the backbone was cushioned by plum-coloured discs that yielded spongily to the end of his pencil.

He saw too that something string-like, as thin as cotton, had started to thread its way through the tunnel of the vertebrae, and angling the beam of the desk lamp through the eye socket he traced it back to the skull. At the rear of the cavity, the string protruded like a single white hair and at its tip grew a grey polyp that under the magnifying glass seemed to be crimped and folded into a tiny brain.

He wanted to bring Juliette into the study and show her. If she wished to put her faith in something, then this was it. But it felt as though all this was for him alone to see. And Juliette was too absorbed in her own thoughts anyway.

Though what she was thinking about was hard to guess. She looked disorientated but at the same time full of a peculiar equanimity. She no longer shut herself away but that didn't mean she wanted to speak to anyone either. Eventually, even Harrie gave up trying and left her to her quiet contemplation.

She still ate very little and that evening she went to sleep in Ewan's room as she had for the last six months but she no longer read stories to thin air or cried out in the night.

The next morning, Richard found the hare's limbs fastened by thicker bands of tendon and the skull strapped with the taut cords that swivelled the eyes and moved the jaw. The hind quarters were packed with heavy fillets of muscle that were cold and moist to the touch. Instead of laying down newspaper over the animal, Richard went to the linen cupboard on the landing and rooted out an old blanket. After carefully wrapping the hare, he laid it back in the cardboard box and set it down next to the radiator.

Incubated by the heat from the ticking pipes, the remains (if they could still be called so) began to give off a sickly smell, like that of a butcher's block, and when Richard looked again later in the day, fat had appeared, gelatinous and yellow, as though the animal had been buttered.

At the next inspection, the upper layer of this jelly had become dry and smooth; and at the next, skin had started to form on the back legs. By midnight, the process was complete and the hare wore a pale jacket that, bald and wrinkled, gave it the look of a creature just born.

Richard spent a restless night on the sofa by the bookshelves and when he came out of the study in the dark of the early morning he found that Juliette had left his portable recorder by the door along with the tapes she'd made.

All that day, she moved about the house with purpose, tidying the front room or cleaning in the kitchen. Still distrustful at the sudden change, Harrie questioned Richard again about what the Beacons had said and done but he had no idea what to tell her. In any case, he didn't think that the difference in Juliette was anything to do with Mrs Forde, but the presence of the hare.

Every time he removed the lid and unpeeled the swaddling there was something new to see. But if he waited for these transformations to occur before his eyes, nothing happened at all and he came to understand that the hare needed the privacy of its cardboard pupa.

While he worked, the animal began to consume his thoughts entirely. As he knelt by the ditch in the tent and felt his thighs aching, he pictured the hare's muscular haunches. As he drew his fingers through the mud and caked his nails with filth, so the hare acquired its claws. They curled out from between the velvety pads of its toes, sharp and black. Not just for scrabbling in the earth but for fighting too, and Richard imagined the hare up on its hind legs in the springtime sparring, its opponent slashed and defeated.

By the evening, the fur of peach-fuzz had thickened to a rich pelt the colour of dry earth.

Whiskers pronged from the snout.

Genitals swelled like little tubers.

The ears unfurled from buds of gristle into tall ragged lugs.

Seeking an explanation for it all seemed ungrateful. A great kindness was at work here and he felt that by questioning the restoration he might jeopardise its fulfilment. He didn't feel confused. He had witnessed what had happened and there it was. He wasn't being asked to wonder, only observe and be awake to what he was being shown. The spring was coming. Soon, there would only be newness.

At dawn the next morning – four days now since Mrs Forde and the Beacons had been – a thrush was whistling just outside the window and its sudden scatter of notes seemed to accelerate the changes in the hare. It troubled Richard that he was finally witness to a process of reconstruction that, until now, had been so confidential, but yet he couldn't look away.

As he sat down to watch, something bubbled up inside one of the eye sockets and, using the magnifying glass again, he saw tiny white beads growing like mould on the optic nerve. They engorged and merged and, as a pearl forms around a speck of grit, an eye grew milky white. For a time the hare looked blind, but after a while there came a gradual bleeding of colour and the blank sclera turned first yellow, then orange before deepening to a dark shade of honey wax. Then, as if a spot of ink had been dropped on to the cornea, the black of the pupil widened and widened until the hare was staring at him.

Richard sat for some time before laying his hand on the animal's flank. It was still cold under the fur. There was no beat of life inside its chest. If he were to lift up the hare it would hang limply. But touching the pelt seemed suddenly like defilement and he took his hand away, hoping that he hadn't brought the hare's revival to a premature end. It seemed prudent to leave it alone for a while longer yet and he gently tucked the blanket around the animal before setting the box down by the radiator again. With some reluctance, he closed the door and went out to the field.

For the rest of the day, as he hunkered inside the tent and worked the trowel into the soil, there was an overwhelming sense of imminence, of things brimming on the cusp.

And when the candle in the kitchen finally went out, everything overflowed.

~

Coming back to the house late in the afternoon, cold and tired, Richard found the hare's blanket empty on the floor of the study.

The sensation of being watched was as strong as the odour of urine and musty fur and as Richard closed the door behind him the hare emerged from under the desk, as large and lithe as a cat.

He moved slowly but the animal darted across the rug to the radiator and doubled back, only to scut away when it caught sight of him again.

Seeking the darkest place it could find, it wedged itself between the end of the bookcase and the filing cabinet, its wet eyes fixed on his, its back legs cocked like a trigger. Richard felt his pulse quickening and his nerves electrified with the anticipation of the hare making a sudden dash towards him out of panic or defence. And so it was with quiet, gradual movements that he crouched down and let his eyes adjust to the gloom.

The hare had not been reborn in a pristine state of health but at the age it must have been when it died. Around the muzzle there was a greyness to the fur and it had the lean face of an animal hardened by the northern seasons. And by loneliness too. A buck hare never had a tribe to rule, he had no dark warren full of family. He lived by his own wits and in doing so acquired a deep wisdom of the world. He knew what men were, what men did.

Dipping its head, but keeping Richard in its gaze, it nibbled at some ancient crumbs on the floor. It was famished. Of course it was.

Downstairs, Richard foraged in the pantry bin for the vegetable scraps left over from the last meal Harrie had made and collected a bowlful of carrot peelings and cabbage leaves. From the shelf where the cereals were kept, he brought down a glass jar of oats.

The hare was where he had left it, still watching, still primed to run. Without getting too close, Richard scattered the food on to the floor. Even though it must have been hungry, the animal wouldn't move and so he sat at the desk and read quietly, hoping that the silence might encourage it out to feed. Some ten or fifteen minutes later, the hare crept forward, crouching low to the rug, its ears flat over its back.

Some of its nervousness had dissipated but it was still twitchy and Richard gave it a reverential berth as he went to watch it from the sofa. He'd sat here with Ewan so many times that the boy was easily conjured up by the sour smell of the leather. But that evening he was muffled and indistinct.

For the last few months Richard had felt as if his mind were constantly falling like water through rocks, split into many streams, each one clattering and ricocheting down and down until he was exhausted. Now there was peace.

He stared into the hare's peeled, polished eye until he fell asleep.

When he woke again, still on the couch, it was to full daylight and the sound of the hare's claws against the window. It raked and scratched, clouding the glass with its breath as it pined after the field and the wood.

Outside, the first true warmth of the year was starting to melt the snow in the front garden. The ash trees dripped and the roofs of the cars on the driveway gave off wisps of evaporating moisture. In the sunlight, wood and stone were polished. It was almost blinding to look along the lane. But it was the birds, thought Richard. The astonishment of them. Down in the wood, they were loud with delight but also shock, as if after the long winter they had found their songs too big for their mouths and could not prevent them from spilling out across the field.

The hare gazed through the window, its eyes following every movement of the world outside. Richard had known since it skinked out from under the desk that it could not stay here long. To keep it locked up in the study would be cruel. The poor creature didn't know that it had been a parable. It just wanted to eat.

But it would have to wait until dusk. To take it back to the field weak from undernourishment and in broad daylight would make it easy prey for the vixen or the rooks. Though the question of how he would get it there was difficult. He didn't think that it would allow itself to be picked up and the box in which it had slept had been torn open in its awakening.

In the shed, behind a stack of fence panels that he had been meaning to break up for the woodstove, Richard found some of the fruit boxes that Juliette used to pick up from Cannon's to use as kindling. Two of them sandwiched together would make a temporary cage and keep the hare contained while he removed it from the house. Yet it was a powerful animal and would be stronger still when it was full of fear and adrenalin. Unless the lid was secured in some way it would easily burst free, so he cut some lengths of wire that he could use to lash the two crates together once the hare was inside. And to get it inside in the first place would not be easy. Harsh though it might be, he would have to make the creature go hungry for a few hours more so that it could be lured by food later.

*

The thaw continued for the rest of the day, calving thick wedges of snow from the roof and sending them tumbling past the windows. In the field, the sun's transit was marked by a wide tract of exposed mud that, by the evening, had a bright sheen of water, making the tent look like an overturned boat. It was six o'clock and the sun was starting to go down. The hare had been restless for hours and now it went to the door again and clawed at the wood. It had waited long enough.

Richard set the crates on their side in the shape of a pincer and laid down a trail of cabbage in order to lead the hare inside. He switched off the desk lamp and the hare lolloped over and sniffed at the leaves, eating as it would in the wild, called back to vigilance every other second, staring, chewing, staring again. In time, it came closer to the crates and sneaked between them to get at the oats. Richard waited until it had bent down for another mouthful and then moved quickly from his chair to close the two boxes together.

Realising that it was caught, the hare panicked, kicking and battering with its back feet. As Richard twisted the wires tight, it began to make a guttural sound and thrust its snout through the holes, its nostrils flaring, its teeth gnawing at the wood. They were sharp enough to make peels and splinters straight away and mindful that his fingers might be next, Richard wrapped the makeshift cage in the hare's blanket before lifting it up.

The animal was even heavier than he had anticipated, and he had to readjust his grip and balance several times as he negotiated the stairs.

Harrie was in the kitchen and, hearing him coming down awkwardly, called, 'Jules? Is that you?' But before she could see him and start asking questions, Richard had opened the front door with his elbow and closed it with his foot.

Compared to the fleeting oxblood sunsets that they'd had all winter, that evening was slow to fade. Over the fells, the moon was still pale and the ridges still tinted by the sun. The air was raw but invigorating and filled the lungs with a purgative coldness.

Richard tried to step around the puddles on the lane but a particularly wide pool was unavoidable and he came to the gate with wet feet. On the other side, the earth had been softened by the melting snow and he had to slow his pace so that he didn't slip. It became impossible to take a straight line and he was made to zigzag down to more even ground, holding the cage close to his chest and trying to keep it level.

Near the tent, he stopped and set the crates down, taking care not to injure the animal. Although its heart was a piston, and it coursed with hot blood, its revival had been dependent on so many intricate miracles that it still seemed fragile.

But now that the hare had sensed its freedom it clawed hard at the wood, making Richard work quicker to undo the wires. As soon as there was a gap, it nosed its way out and headed for the first clear line of sight it could find, which was back towards the house. Before it could get too far, Richard clapped his hands and the hare turned around and sprinted off towards Croften Wood, opening its long lean body into full flight.

Richard watched it for as long as he could before it disappeared into the trees.

He doubted that he'd see much of it again. There was nothing for it to eat out here in the field. It would find a dark den in the hogweed and the brambles, then if it had any sense it would cross the beck and go up to the Westburys' hayfield. Come the summer, the ryegrass and cat's tail would grow around it as thick as a forest.

For a few minutes more, he looked to catch a last glimpse of the animal, but it had become one of the itinerant shadows that moved as the wind caught the trees. It had returned to patterns of living that were impossible to understand: where every movement and every sound meant something and nothing could be ignored; not the twitch of a leaf or the odour of earth or the sound of birds conversing across the wood. But Richard wondered if the hare in some way felt as he did that spring was always *bestowed*. That it was an invitation to come and watch the world moving and be among its tremors. Here in the field, those first shocks of the season were starting now. He could feel them and hear them. Beneath the trills and whistles of the blackbirds he became aware of a rushing sound. It was the beck flowing again, released from its rictus of ice.

~

Over the winter, he'd been able to walk a good half a mile along its length without once hearing it creak or crack. It was the same every year. Ewan had always thought it quite a thrill to stand in the middle of the stream and feel it concrete-hard under his feet. But by the end of his first term at school, he didn't want to do anything like that any more. At home he was distant; in class, sullen and lethargic, and – his teacher complained – completely unwilling to participate in the rehearsals for the nativity play.

Her opinion of Ewan coloured by what had happened with Susan Drewitt, Richard assumed that young Miss Clarke was exaggerating, but on the afternoon of the performance in the school hall, Ewan had made for a decidedly listless shepherd. While the others were earnestly proffering their lambs to the Christ-child he stood by the wings raking the bottom of his crook against the stage. He took no bow at the end of 'O Come, All Ye Faithful' and stayed silent on the journey home, despite Richard and Juliette's attempts at praise.

The holidays came around, the temperature fell sharply, and, with a great deal of persuasion, Richard managed to get Ewan to come and see the frozen beck. Of course, once he was actually there, he enjoyed himself just as much as Richard had promised he would. He skidded on the ice, tested its firmness with jumps and kicks, took pleasure at hearing the sound of his voice echoing in the winter wood. Then, as they walked back up to the house for lunch, it started snowing and Ewan let go of Richard's hand and ran this way and that, trying to catch the flakes.

By the late afternoon, the whole of Croftendale was covered and Richard and Juliette took Ewan back to the field to build a snowman.

Perhaps it was purely the novelty of finding the place so altered by the weather, but it wasn't long before the boy seemed to rediscover the joy of playing there.

It was school, Richard thought. That was at the root of his unhappiness. It couldn't suit every child. Especially a child like Ewan, who struggled to keep pace with his peers. In a small place like Holy Cross, it was more noticeable too. Perhaps it might be better to enrol him in one of the bigger primaries in Skipton? Or even for Juliette to teach him at home? But he knew that she would be resistant to either of those suggestions. For her, the village school was one of the details that affirmed the goodness of country living, along with the ribbons at the spring fair, the sound of faint Sunday church bells, white sheep on green hillsides, and this – their own field deep in snow two days before Christmas.

The ball that she and Ewan had been rolling down the slope had congealed into a sizeable boulder by the time it was on flat ground. They rubbed and patted it smooth, while Richard made the snowman's head. Naturally, Juliette had come prepared and from the pockets of her duffle coat she handed Ewan a carrot and some pieces of coal she'd taken from the bucket by the fire. Richard lifted him up and he assembled the face, carefully studding in the mouth until it was the proper shape of a smile. Now all the fellow needed was a hat and scarf, and Richard was badgered from both sides until he parted with the ones he was wearing. His protest against the idea had seemed perfectly legitimate: surely a snowman had to stay cold in order for him not to become a puddle? But Ewan gave him a derisive look – it was identical to Juliette's – and logic was trumped by aesthetics.

'He's got to be dressed, Daddy.'

'Even if it means I freeze?'

Ewan shrugged. Rules were rules. And after the ensuing snowball fight Richard trudged back to the house unable to feel his ears and neck.

In front of the fire with a glass of Scotch, the chill subsided, but Juliette wanted to play nurse and he'd happily let her. She rubbed the feeling back into his hands and after putting Ewan to bed filled the bath for two. The moment of contentment he felt as she took off her dressing gown and lay back against him in the hot water continued for the rest of the night. Actually, it was more than contentment. It was the relief of not having to think about Ewan's future for the time being. That afternoon in the field had proved that he could still be happy. He could still seem like their little boy.

They washed one another, dried themselves, made love, and slept with an easy quietness. Juliette rested properly for the first time in weeks and didn't even stir when Ewan got up early the next morning and went downstairs.

Richard lay in bed and listened to him creeping about in the hallway and then opening and closing the front door with the stealth of a departing burglar.

Going to the window, he watched Ewan high-stepping through the snow in his wellingtons. Rather endearingly, he paused by the lane to check if there were any cars coming, even though it was the deathly silent morning of Christmas Eve and the tarmac was under a two-foot drift.

In bed, Juliette gave a long inward breath and stretched out under the blanket. Richard was glad when she lay still again. If she'd seen Ewan, she would have been banging on the window and telling him to come inside. It was better that the boy was left to go and explore. Wasn't that exactly what Juliette wanted? For him to be a country lad who went out on winter mornings and was taught as much (if not more) among the fields and fells and woods as he was in the classroom.

Down the slope, Ewan followed the line of the trench he and Juliette had peeled open during the construction of the snowman the day before and stood in the giant's bulky shadow. From there he carried on to the bounds of the wood, picking up fallen sticks. The snowman needed arms. Perhaps a besom too.

The deadfall gathered, Ewan retraced his boot holes and dumped the bundle at his feet. As he separated what he'd collected, he seemed compelled to look behind him towards the middle of the field as if he were half seeing the oak tree again, as if it loomed over him.

From the pile on the ground, he selected a long branch and snapped it in half over his knee as he'd seen Richard do to make kindling.

As he moved around to the side of the snowman, he stumbled a little and got up again, adjusting his bobble hat so that he could see where he was inserting the stick. With both hands he drove it into the snowman's shoulder but didn't stop until it had come out of the other side. He did the same with the other branches, ramming each one through the torso and turning the snowman into St Sebastian. Then, taking the two ends of Richard's scarf, he pulled until the head was severed and fell to the ground.

Richard would have kept Juliette away from the window, but she'd got out of bed so quietly that he hadn't noticed she was up until she was next to him, tugging the other curtain aside. By then, Ewan was breaking the carrot nose and stamping out the smile.

It was nothing, he said to her. Ewan was only doing to the snowman what children enjoyed doing to their own sandcastles. But she was already getting dressed.

'You let him go out on his own?' she said. 'You watched him do that?'

In her coat and boots, she crossed the lane to the field and he followed her, repeating what he'd said in the bedroom. She was overreacting. There was nothing wrong. It'd be best to leave him be. But on reaching Ewan, Juliette took hold of his arm and smacked his backside until he cried as hard as she thought he ought to do. Trying to get between them, Richard did his best to reason with her, but she was too incensed and distraught to listen and dragged the boy back through the snow to the house.

~

There was no point hoping to see the hare any more now that it was dark, and Richard picked up the two boxes he'd used to remove the animal from the study. They stank of sour urine and had been scratched and chewed enough in places for the wood to have given way. A good thing that he hadn't had to go very far. Still, the show of strength was exhilarating. He'd rarely come so close to such brute energy. He was glad to have seen the potency he'd imagined in the bones released with such an emphatic burst. There must have been joy in it for the hare too. To have known itself again; to have given itself back to the dark.

While Richard had been listening to the trickle of the beck, the moon had cleared the tree tops and the night was turning star-rich. He didn't want to go back to the house just yet and went to the tent to work, leaving the flaps open so that he could have the evening inside with him.

With the gas lamp purring, he moved to the other side of the hole and continued to dig carefully with the edge of the trowel. At the third or fourth pass the blade bit down and chipped off a sliver of something hard. Smoothing off the mud with his thumb, Richard saw that it was a small piece of wood and, gouging in the hole with his fingers, he felt a length of root just under the surface of the soil.

For the next hour, he raked away at the earth, lying on his belly to scoop out a cavity, scraping off the filth with his hands.

The root ran diagonally through the rectangle, discoloured by the blackness of mud and time. Whether it had belonged to the Stythwaite Oak was impossible to tell at first glance. So little was known about what had actually happened here over the last few centuries that the history of the field was mostly guesswork. It seemed infertile now, but how long had that been the case? There was nothing to say that another tree couldn't have grown and died here at some point. A sample of what he'd exposed would have to be taken for dating to be absolutely sure, but if it were part of the Oak, then he must still have been digging some way out from the trunk. The root was not particularly substantial, given the tree's purported size. It must have tapered down at this point from a much greater girth.

This was his strategy then: to trace each stem he found back to its source as far as he could and little by little try to pinpoint where the tree might once have grown.

After wiping his hands on his jeans, he jotted down some notes in the book and wrote: 'ill equipped, Willoughby!' – underlining it twice. It was true. He had no camera with him, no maps on which to plot what he'd found. It had taken him by surprise. The dig had been a distraction, and actually unearthing something had suddenly made it all complicated.

He sat for a while looking at the root, planning where he would search next. Might he need a second tent? Some extra tarpaulin to stake out over each new plot he made? How would he keep the roots from drying out? He felt that he should contact Stella and get her opinion; this was her area of expertise.

She was a good strategist, too, and he knew that she would encourage him to use what he'd found to his advantage and play the university powers at their own game. They'd called his temporary expulsion 'research leave' but hadn't really expected him to do anything other than mourn for Ewan. If he could show them that in fact he'd been doing exactly what they'd told him to do with his time, then they could have little reason to keep him away any longer. There would have to be some reward for his obedience.

He knew that Stella would fight his corner on that score, but not without some reassurances about

Juliette. She would want to know that she was well enough to be left alone when Richard returned to campus.

Juliette was different; he could say that. But how he'd phrase the way in which she'd changed would take some thought. Her behaviour was so odd. He had noticed in her something of the nesting instinct she'd had before Ewan was born, but it was much more erractic. He'd find her repairing something – a door handle, a broken plate – and then five minutes later she'd be out in the garden weeding one of the beds. She'd have the radio on over-loud in the kitchen as she mopped the floor, and by the time he'd gone down to switch it off she'd be making her way slowly along the hallway in silent meditation. He tried to talk to her on all such occasions, but she gave no response other than a calm smile. Could he say, then, that she was happy?

When he came back to the house, Harrie was at the front door looking for him.

'It's Juliette,' she said, when he came inside.

'What about her? What's wrong?'

'Go on,' she said, looking at the stairs. 'Go and see.'

He went up with Harrie behind him.

'Keep going,' she said, when they came to the first landing.

Above him on the upper floor he could hear Juliette walking over the bare boards and the sound of things being moved about. When he came to Ewan's room, the door was propped open with one of his larger teddy bears and Juliette was taking down the old boxes of jigsaws from the top of the dresser.

'They're always looking for donations at the church,' she said, and went back to what she was doing.

Harrie touched Richard's shoulder and whispered in his ear.

'Go and wash your hands. And then come and help.'

Over the course of the evening, talking only about the practicalities of what they were doing, they removed the mattress Juliette had been sleeping on and took all the mirrors back to the rooms where they belonged. Harrie stripped Ewan's bed and carried the sheets downstairs to be washed along with the clothes that had been hanging in the wardrobe for the last six months. Gloves were reunited, little woolly hats dusted off. Shoes went into a carrier bag and sat against the wall like a sack of potatoes.

Exactly what had made Juliette choose to start this now, Richard couldn't work out. All evening he'd been waiting for her to realise the enormity of her decision and call the process to a halt, but it seemed as though, having embarked on the task, she wanted to complete it quickly and thoroughly. He had surprised himself too. Spending more time in Ewan's room than he had for months, he'd expected to be tormented. But with the spring here memories had truly started to feel like the stuff of the past. When the boy came to him now, it was not with the same intensity. Rather than smothering him, he lingered at the edge of his thoughts, which was the proper place for the dead. The only place. And returning the room to a shell would keep him there.

'I'll start on the toys, shall I?' said Richard and knelt down by the window to collect up the litter of dice and playing cards, conkers and dominoes.

The dressing-up clothes were all stuffed into a wicker chest and could stay that way. The child who received them next would not want everything neatly matched. They would enjoy pulling things out at random, as Ewan had done, and pair a space suit with an Apache headdress, or run around the garden half Zorro, half Robin Hood.

With the basket out on the landing, Richard went about the room picking up the other odds and ends

– the cars and bricks and rubber dinosaurs. Finally, he crouched down by the train set and started to pack it away, removing the little station and the water tower, uncoupling the engine from its fleet of yellow hoppers. The track came up piece by piece until only the shape of it remained, outlined with dust on the rug.

He closed the box, sealed it with tape and wrote on the lid with a marker pen. Soon, there were other boxes lined up against the wall – BOOKS, TEDDY BEARS, GAMES, CARS – which they carried down to the scullery.

'We could take some things to the church tomorrow,' said Juliette and Harrie agreed.

'If you like,' she said and then, tentatively, making it seem off-hand, she suggested that the toys might actually go to the children's ward at the infirmary.

'You could take them when you go back to work,' she said.

'Yes,' said Juliette. 'I suppose I could.'

By midnight, Ewan's room had been emptied but for the rocking chair and the little wooden bed. Juliette swept and hoovered and Harrie cleaned the grime from the windows. All that was left to do was remove the name glued to the door and Richard prised off the E, W, A and N with a screwdriver.

One by one, the three of them came to the end of their individual tasks and went out on to the landing.

'God, I'm ravenous,' said Juliette. 'Is it too late to eat?'

'Not at all,' said Harrie. 'What would you like? I'll make whatever you want. Just tell me.'

'Anything. Everything.'

'All right,' said Harrie, heading down to the kitchen. 'There'll be something on the table whenever you're ready.'

'There is some white paint left in the shed, isn't there, Richard?' said Juliette.

'I think so, yes,' he replied.

'I'd like it all white,' she said, looking into the bare box of the room. 'Like it used to be.'

'Fine.'

'We could get it done tomorrow. Me and Harrie.'

'If that's what you want.'

'It is,' said Juliette, and switched off the light. 'I want it to look like a nursery.'

Richard imagined her pregnant again, all breasts and belly. Carrying a girl this time. The seed of the family proper.

Ewan would still be here with them, of course. There would be photographs to show and stories to tell their Linda, Jason, Bobby and Jo as soon as they were old enough to understand that death had been to Starve Acre and that was the way of things sometimes.

Death came, but it went again.

And perhaps Juliette had realised at last that she needn't be so submissive to it any more. There was no reason why they couldn't make Starve Acre the centre of Willoughby life just as they'd always planned.

Richard felt the past receding like a tide. The hare had brought the spring. The worst of their grief was over. Perhaps they had survived.

Part Two

Although she had gutted Ewan's room, it was still too soon for Juliette to remove herself completely. She spent the night on the boy's bed and slept well. Richard too. There had been no shake of his shoulder; no Juliette whispering in his ear about the footsteps she'd heard on the landing or the small voice singing in the garden.

In the morning she was up before he was and he found her talking to Harrie in what he supposed he now ought to call the nursery again. Part of him flared with the anxiety that she had changed her mind overnight, but the clearance had been so complete that to put everything back now would be an even more arduous task. And what would be the point? The mess could never be perfectly reassembled.

'I'll go and fetch the brushes,' said Harrie and went downstairs.

'I suppose we should move the cot back in here,' Juliette said. 'I could give it a coat of paint once the walls are done.'

Richard agreed, happy to let her dictate the pace, and followed her to the master bedroom, where for several years Ewan's old hand-built crib had been sitting against the wall and waiting to be filled. When they were inside, Juliette put her hand on his shoulder and for a moment he thought she might close the door, turn the key and want to . . . But she went over to the cot and tested its weight.

'It's heavier than I remember,' she said.

With Richard pulling and Juliette pushing, they managed to move the solid pine crate across the landing and to the middle of the nursery where it had stood when Ewan was a baby.

Harrie came back up the stairs wearing an old shirt of Juliette's and carrying cans of emulsion.

'Let's do this wall first,' said Juliette, smoothing her hand over the cartoon.

'Are you sure?' said Harrie. 'After all the work you put into it.'

'I don't care,' said Juliette. 'I want everything gone.'

Harrie kissed her on the cheek and they started by painting over the dragon that lived in the clouds.

*

In the study, Richard wound a sheet of paper into the typewriter and began a letter to Stella. He chose his words carefully, outlining what he'd found in the field, though making no mention of the hare.

He came to the end of what he could say about the Stythwaite Oak for the moment and read over what he'd written. A few amendments were needed. He took a red pen and underlined the sentences that could be phrased more clearly.

Setting the sheet aside, he inserted a blank and typed 'Juliette is better' before backtracking over the last word with xs and using 'well' instead. 'Juliette is well,' he put. 'She seems to have turned a corner. She might think about going back to work soon.' But compared to what he'd said about the excavation in the field it was too impassive. Stella would know that he was hiding something.

The paper balled in the bin, Richard started the page again and then a third time and eventually got up from the desk to think about how best to explain the sudden switch in Juliette's mind. As he considered the problem, he searched for the set of large-scale geological maps he remembered his father owning. If the university allowed him back, he'd be teaching the course on Neolithic Britain in the summer term and the maps would be useful.

After scouring the shelves and some of the boxes, Richard looked through the stacks of random books by the window. He set aside a few lucky finds on Doggerland and flint-knapping and in shaking out the contents of a large envelope he discovered another of the woodblock prints.

The scene this time was of a Hanging Day. Three men dangled from the bough.

Here was Roderick Sayles: He Burned The Hay.

Next to him an Edmund Calvert, Who Befpoiled A Corpfe.

The last, suspended closest to the trunk, was Will Beeston – Ecstafie His Mafter – whose offence, deemed the worst, floated in pictorial form in a cloud above the onlookers. He was shown at the top of the church tower saying, See How This Angel Flyes, as he threw a child from the parapet.

The dead men, bound at the wrists, their heads yanked aside sharply in the nooses, did not seem particularly old. They were boys, really, when Richard looked more closely. The Bonnie Sonnes of the three farmers in the previous engraving.

It seemed that the whole village had turned out to watch the executions and were gathered around the tree like the spectators in *Foxe's Book of Martyrs*. And while there were often a few onlookers weeping in these types of scenes, Richard had never seen an outpouring of tears on a scale like this.

It appeared that the three boys had been put to death with great reluctance.

Richard was collecting his camera equipment from the cupboard in the scullery when Juliette came in to wash her hands.

'You've finished already?' he said.

'One coat's done. We're just letting it dry.'

She ran the tap and let the water steam. There was white paint up her arms, smeared across her forehead. In those days and weeks after they'd first moved here, she'd looked the same. She'd worn the same shirt then too, one of his cast-offs. The top three or four buttons were undone, exposing her bony chest. Noticing a spatter of paint there, she wetted her fingers and rubbed at the top of her breasts.

'Why now?' Richard said, diverting his attention to the boxes of film on the shelf.

'Sorry?'

'Ewan's room,' said Richard. 'What made you want to empty it?'

'I thought that was what you wanted?'

149

'I wasn't criticising.'

She worked soap vigorously up her forearms.

'I can't think why I would keep the room as it was,' she said. 'Not now.'

'Because of what Mrs Forde said?'

'Because of what she showed me.'

'Which was?'

Juliette glanced at him and rinsed the lather off her hands.

'Didn't you see anything?' she said.

'You know I didn't.'

'Nothing at all? You passed the blood test.'

'For what it was worth.'

Instead of contempt, she had only sympathy for him. 'I'm sorry you missed out,' she said.

She dried her hands. The patch of skin on her chest glistened.

'What happened?' said Richard. 'I still don't understand.'

'There isn't anything to understand.'

'So everyone keeps telling me.'

'It'll be clear to you soon.'

'Can't you try to explain it?'

She hung the towel on the peg by the door, then put her hands on Richard's waist and searched his eyes. It was the first intimate touch she'd given him since Ewan died.

'What's wrong?' she said.

When he couldn't say, she said, 'I feel better, Richard. I thought you'd be happy.'

'I am.'

'Well then.'

She reached up and kissed him on the mouth. The way she tasted was unfamiliar, but then it had been a while. He put his hands on her lower back and drew her closer, stiffening at the press of her body. She felt it, closed her eyes, but then pulled away from him, touched his face and went through the kitchen to the stairs.

He'd suspected for some time that to feel desire of that kind would be a gradual process for her. It would happen when she was ready to think about having children again, and she wasn't at that point yet. Not really. When he thought about them bringing up another child, a different child, at Starve Acre and tried to cast Juliette in the role of mother again he couldn't quite picture it. She was still putting herself back together. Emptying Ewan's room was a move forward, but it was only the first of a hundred steps.

*

Closing the front door, Richard went down to the driveway. On the lane, he heard Gordon's van approaching and he waited for him to pull in.

'Richard,' he said, winding down the window. 'I've caught you on the hop, haven't I? Sorry. How's Juliette been?'

'Earnest.'

'Oh?'

'Or thorough. I'm not quite sure what the right word is.'

'Has something happened?

'She's cleared Ewan's room.'

Gordon got out of the van and closed the door. 'I told you she'd be a changed person.'

'I still don't understand what she saw,' Richard said. 'She won't tell me.'

'That's because it's not really something you can tell someone else. It's not communicable in that way. There are certain things . . . it's not always possible . . .'

His answer drifted. There was clearly something on his mind but he put off disclosing what it was for a while longer by noting the bag of equipment in Richard's hand.

'You look industrious,' he said.

'I've found some of the roots,' said Richard.

'You're not serious? And they belong to the Oak, do they?'

'As far as I can tell.'

'In that case, I'd shovel the soil back into the hole and leave them to the dark.'

'I'm not sure the university would be happy if I did that,' said Richard. 'What's wrong?'

Gordon was looking at the house again, not really listening.

'It's Mrs Forde,' he said. 'She's the reason I've not been able to come and see you until today. She's still very unwell after the other night.'

'Is she?'

A little taken aback, Gordon said, 'You don't seem particularly concerned, Richard.'

'It was an act, Gordon. I got it.'

'It wasn't an act,' he said.

'So, what was wrong with her then?'

'I'm not sure. I've never seen her like this before. It's strange.'

Gordon seemed to be groping for words. He didn't look well himself. The skin around his eyes was puffy and sore as though he hadn't slept properly for days.

'Look, I know you'll scoff,' he said. 'But I wouldn't be able to forgive myself if I didn't tell you what she told me.'

'Which was what?'

The effort of trying to phrase it all in the right way seemed to be paining him.

'She sensed something in the house,' he said eventually.

'Something?' said Richard. 'Like what?'

'She couldn't say exactly. Something unpleasant.'

'Unpleasant?'

'Fetid was the word she used.'

'What was it? A smell?'

'She said it was hard to make out.'

'Well, it all sounds appropriately vague,' said Richard.

It was the response that Gordon seemed to have expected. 'I told her you'd be derisive,' he said.

'Are you surprised?'

'You still feel that way?' Gordon said. 'Even though Juliette's better?'

'I didn't say she was better.'

Frustrated, Gordon said, 'Richard, you and Juliette are such good friends. I just don't want to see you hurt.'

'Hurt? How?'

Gordon looked at him squarely. 'Whatever it is you've brought into your home,' he said, 'get rid of it.'

'Is this a trick?' said Richard. 'So Juliette will have to invite that woman back to cleanse the house or something?'

'Why on earth would we want to trick you?' Gordon said.

Richard didn't say so, but he knew that people like Mrs Forde could only exist as long as others believed that they were gifted in some occult way. Without devotees, they would be nothing. They fed off people like Juliette.

'Richard, I doubt that Mrs Forde would ever come back here anyway,' said Gordon. 'The poor woman was shaking by the time I got her home.'

'It was a consummate performance, then.'

Gordon shook his head and made a move towards the front steps.

'Perhaps I could talk to Juliette,' he said. 'She might want to listen at least.'

'No,' said Richard, holding his arm. 'I don't want Juliette hearing any of this. She's been through enough.'

'But she needs to know.'

'Is this what you lot do? You giveth and you taketh away?'

'You must see that I'm only trying to help,' said Gordon. 'I care about Juliette very much.'

'Then leave her alone,' said Richard. 'Let her mind settle. Please.'

He opened the door of the van and after a moment Gordon got back inside.

Through the window, he said, 'Stay away from the field, Richard. I know you think I'm being ridiculous about what happened to your father, but he spent a lot of time there. And so did Ewan.'

'You're right,' said Richard. 'You are being ridiculous.'

Gordon looked over to the house. 'Whatever your opinion of me,' he said, 'you can't deny that the boy changed. You and I were both there.'

'When?' said Richard.

It was deliberately hostile; he couldn't help himself.

But Gordon was too weary to respond and backed out on to the lane without saying anything more. His expression communicated enough: that Richard knew exactly what he was talking about.

~

Throughout Ewan's first term at school, Juliette had kept everything that had happened from her parents, but during the Christmas holidays, on Boxing Day afternoon, Richard heard her sobbing down the phone to her mother and telling her about the incident with Susan Drewitt, the fire, the hacked-up snowman.

Eileen and Doug had been due to go to friends on New Year's Eve but they said that they would cancel and drive down to Starve Acre instead. Juliette's mother wasn't one to miss an opportunity to take charge. She would have no qualms about chastising the boy herself, and her presumption would be that any resistance on his part would be down to haphazard parenting rather than her own bullish manner.

It wasn't at all what Ewan needed and so Richard persuaded Juliette to invite Gordon and Russell too. Eileen was less likely to play the authoritarian in front of strangers.

Now that it seemed as though they'd be having a party, Ewan started negotiating a later bedtime.

'New Year's Eve is no different,' said Juliette. 'It'll be just the same as any other night.'

'You'll only be bored,' said Richard. 'Lots of old people talking. I'm not even sure I want to be there.'

Ewan took a moment to work out if he were being sincere and then returned to the business at hand.

'I won't be bored,' he said in the tone of a promise.

'Don't argue,' said Juliette. 'Daddy's right.'

If he were bored, then he would find some undesirable entertainment. Richard knew exactly what she was thinking.

'I'll be bored in bed,' said Ewan, folding his arms.

'We could give him a bit more time,' said Richard, but Juliette cut short Ewan's smile of victory.

'No,' she said. 'Bed at seven as usual.'

Ewan made a face and said, 'Please. Just for once.'

'Don't whine.'

'Please, Mummy,' Ewan said, and Richard watched Juliette start at the epithet. He hadn't imagined it. She had actually flinched.

She looked away and repeated her answer. 'I said no.'

'I'll be helpful,' said Ewan.

He knew that 'being helpful' was one of the virtues his mother favoured and followed up with more.

'I'll be friendly. I'll speak nicely.'

How soon children learned to barter, Richard thought.

'Please, Mummy. Please,' he said and there was now a little desperation in his voice.

'All right, all right,' said Juliette. 'If it's really that important to you then fine.'

But the gesture that she sent Richard's way told him that if things went wrong, he'd be the one picking up the pieces.

After spitting on their palms, Richard and Ewan shook on half past nine and the boy thought himself very grown up. But then any time after his usual hour would seem to him like the middle of the night.

'Why don't you be the butler for the evening?' Richard suggested, trying to placate Juliette's unease by ensuring that Ewan would be kept occupied. 'You can take people's coats and go around with the crisps and cakes. How about that?'

The idea appealed to him and on the night itself he stood by the front door in his dickie bow an hour before anyone was due to arrive.

Richard brought in more wood for the fire and Juliette busied herself in the kitchen, though she couldn't help but worry that while they were both distracted Ewan would take the opportunity to cause some damage to the house or himself.

'I just don't want Mum and Dad turning up to chaos,' she said. 'They think I'm useless enough as it is.'

Richard put his hands on her hips and kissed the back of her neck. 'Nobody thinks that.'

'Don't they?'

'Only you.'

'Ewan's gone very quiet,' she said, putting down the butter knife and looking along the hallway. 'What's he doing?'

Richard went to see and found the boy peering through the glass panel of the front door with his hands cupped around his face. A car went past outside and though Richard knew that it was Audrey Cannon, he let Ewan enjoy the momentary excitement of thinking that it might be their guests. When the headlights faded, he came away disappointed and Richard stroked his hair.

'They won't be long now,' he said. 'You just keep an ear out for them, Willoughby.'

Ewan straightened his back as butlers were supposed to do and reassumed the posture every time Juliette sent Richard through the hall on a spurious errand.

He'd been rooting out a set of sherry glasses that they wouldn't need from the cabinet under the coat rack when Gordon and Russell knocked. Ewan sprang to attention, draping a tea towel over his arm and bowing as he let them in. Russell laughed and Gordon greased Ewan's palm with a fifty pence piece once the boy had taken his jacket and scarf.

'And where does one get a drink, my man?' he asked.

'A pair of teeths will be surfed in the draw-wring room,' Ewan said, before opening the door to the lounge.

Ten minutes later, he was called into service again when Juliette's parents came in, thrashing out the endgame of an argument about the route they should have taken from the motorway. Doug shook Richard's hand and rolled his eyes as Eileen untoggled her coat, still insisting that she was right: her way would have been quicker.

'And who's this, then?' he said, putting his hands behind his back and looking at Ewan.

'Willoughby, sir.'

'Are you new?'

'We've hired him for the evening,' said Richard.

Doug played along, delighted, and dipped into his pocket for a tip. Eileen seemed wary of the boy, however, and only smiled thinly at him, as she did

161

with Richard, before going to find Juliette in the kitchen.

She closed the door and they spoke alone while Richard and the others sat in the front room to play rummy and charades.

When they both reappeared a while later, Juliette did her best to appear happy as she handed the platter of sandwiches to Ewan but Richard could see that she had been crying. Eileen took a seat near the fire and looked Richard over as she lit a cigarette. Thankfully, Gordon engaged her in conversation and Richard was able to speak to Juliette on her own when she sat down next to him.

'What's wrong?' he said. 'What were you talking about in the kitchen for so long?'

'Nothing.'

'You both sat there in silence, did you?'

Ewan presented them with the mound of sandwiches and they each took one before he was called away by Doug, who wanted Willoughby to fetch in the bottle of Bowmore.

'What do you think we were talking about?' said Juliette.

'And?'

'And we've failed, Richard.'

'Failed how?'

'We should have told her earlier about what's been going on.'

Now Eileen's looks made sense. Given the clandestine nature of the phone call Juliette had made on Boxing Day, she'd come to the conclusion that it was Richard who'd insisted on keeping things from her.

'Well, she knows now,' he said.

'It doesn't matter. She was left out. You know what she's like. They're all the same, Richard. I'll no doubt get it in the neck from Harrie as well when Mum tells her everything.'

'I thought you'd moved from Edinburgh to get away from the McPherson Stasi?' said Richard. 'It's got nothing to do with Harrie. Nor your mother for that matter.'

'She is Ewan's grandma,' said Juliette, chewing the edge of her sandwich. 'She does care about him. She thinks we ought to take him to see Dr Ellis again.'

'For what?'

'To make sure everything's all right.'

'Does he look ill to you?'

'Not physically. That's not what Mum's saying.'

'Oh, upstairs she means. I didn't realise she was a psychiatrist.'

'Do you have to be so sarcastic? She's only trying to help.'

'Well, come on,' he said. 'Ewan's not like that.'

'You can hardly say that he's the same as the others in his class.'

'No, he's not. Thank God.'

The conversation paused as Ewan came around again with the sandwiches. When he'd moved on to Russell, Richard said, 'I don't see how your mum can have any kind of opinion about him anyway. She hardly ever sees him.'

'She was a teacher for thirty years,' said Juliette. 'She knows what she's talking about when it comes to kids.'

'He's only just five,' said Richard. 'Give him a chance.'

'Aye,' Juliette replied. 'Mum said that you were in denial.'

Even though Ewan had agreed to go to bed at nine thirty, when the time came he refused and Eileen looked on as though she hadn't expected anything less of him. Richard made light of it and swept the boy on to his shoulders, jigging him up the stairs to his room and singing 'The Grand Old Duke of York' over the cries of protest.

The promise of stories persuaded him to clean his teeth and put on his pyjamas and then after 'Rumpelstiltskin' and 'The Cat in the Hat' he at last began to look drowsy.

Richard kissed him on the forehead and Ewan wrapped his arms around his neck, squeezing until it became uncomfortable.

'What's the matter?' asked Richard.

'Will it be noisy in the field tonight?' said Ewan.

'Why would it be noisy?'

Ewan let go. 'He says my name sometimes. He tells me to come to the tree.'

'Who does?'

'Jack Grey.'

'Jack Grey?' said Richard. 'Where did you hear about him? From Gordon?'

Ewan seemed to think that it would be a betrayal to say yes out loud and so he nodded instead.

'And what does he sound like, this Jack Grey?' asked Richard.

'I don't like remembering his voice.'

'Well, *when* does he talk to you, then? When you're about to go to sleep?'

'Sometimes.'

'What does he say?'

'To do things.'

'Like what?'

'He said to hurt Susan.'

'Did he?'

'He said to break the snowman. He said he didn't like it being there in the field.'

'Is that why you didn't want to go to bed tonight? Because of Jack Grey?'

Ewan nodded again and Richard sat down on the bed.

'You know, Jack Grey isn't real,' he said. 'He's like the Jabberwocky. You don't think the Jabberwocky's real, do you?'

They shared a little laughter at the thought and Ewan shook his head, but it was only to please. It was clear that the boy wasn't at all reassured.

'If you hear him when you're nearly asleep, then I reckon you're just dreaming about him,' said Richard.

'I'm not, Daddy.'

'You might not notice that you are.'

'Daddy, I'm always awake when he talks.'

It was pointless trying to convince him otherwise.

'How about I put the radio on?' said Richard.

Ewan liked the foreign longwave stations. The incomprehensible murmurings from Göteborg or

Hilversum had always sent the boy to sleep when he was little and had had a Pavlovian effect ever since.

Richard plugged in the console, tuned into something he didn't understand and lowered the volume to a soporific level.

'Close your eyes now,' he said and laid an extra blanket over the boy.

Ewan gave an agitated cry – the kind he'd made as a baby – and reached out for him again.

'I'll only be downstairs,' said Richard but the boy clung to him for a while longer.

'Listen,' said Richard. 'You go to sleep and when you wake up in the morning it'll be a brand-new year. All those things that you've been afraid of won't be there any more. I promise.'

When Richard went back to the living room, Gordon broke off from his conversation with Eileen.

'Dr Willoughby,' he said, pouring a fresh glass of wine. 'It's New Year's Eve and you're as dry as a witch's tit. Here.'

He passed over the drink with a look of concern.

'You seem perturbed,' he said. 'Is everything all right?'

'Didn't he settle?' asked Juliette.

'He's fine,' said Richard.

Had he been on his own with Gordon, he would have asked him exactly what kind of stories he'd been telling Ewan. It was one thing spinning him a few yarns, but to keep him awake with thoughts of Jack Grey was too much.

They played Yahtzee, blackjack and whist with the wireless on low in the background and the clock marking off the last hours of the year. Sitting between Gordon and Eileen, who both got louder with every glass they drained, Juliette's restlessness seemed all the more acute. She desperately wanted to go and make sure that Ewan was all right but when she finally got up to do so, her mother guessed her intentions immediately and told her to sit down.

'Just leave him be,' she said, choosing a card from the fan in her hand. 'The more you make a fuss of him, the more he'll act up.'

Gordon rubbed Juliette's arm affectionately and she re-joined the game, her foot tapping anxiously on the floor.

Midnight approached. Eileen topped up the drinks clumsily and licked Beaujolais off the stem of her wine glass. Doug mixed himself another whisky and soda.

On the radio, Big Ben began to toll. There were handshakes and kisses and they linked arms as Gordon started on 'Auld Lang Syne'. When it rolled on through a second chorus and then a third, Juliette took the opportunity to slip out and check on Ewan.

They were still singing when Richard heard her padding down the stairs. She came into the front room distressed, her arm half inside the sleeve of her coat.

'It's Ewan,' she said. 'He's not in the house.'

Doug laughed and poured himself another drink. 'Playing hide and seek, is he? Cheeky bugger.'

'Are you sure he's not in his room?' said Eileen.

'Yes I'm sure,' Juliette replied, sitting down to put on her boots. 'I've looked for him everywhere.'

'He won't have gone outside, will he?' said Gordon. 'It's pitch black and freezing cold.'

'Well, if he's not in the house, Gordon . . .' said Juliette. 'Look, are you going to help me or just stand there?'

Unconvinced that Juliette had searched the house properly, Eileen sent Doug to scour each room and he ambled off with his glass of Scotch. The rest of them went out with torches, to the back garden first and then

169

down the lane. It was a clear night and a freezing easterly wind passed through the trees along the valley.

'He won't go that far,' said Gordon. 'He'll feel the cold and come back soon enough.'

'But we've no idea how long he's been out,' Juliette said. 'If you'd just let me go and check on him, Mum . . .'

'I really don't see how any of this is my fault,' said Eileen. 'Perhaps you ought to keep the front door locked at night.'

'It was locked,' said Richard. 'And bolted.'

'Then I'm surprised we didn't hear him leave,' Russell said.

'Children are more cunning than you think,' said Eileen, but thankfully Juliette wasn't listening and walked away shouting for Ewan. The further along the lane she went the more agitated her voice became.

'Should we call the police?' said Russell.

'I could get in the van and drive down to the village, see if he's there,' Gordon suggested. 'I'm sure I'm sober enough by now.'

'You don't think he'll have gone the other way on to the moors, do you?' said Russell.

But scanning the field with the torch, Richard had lighted on something moving towards them. It was

Ewan, tramping up through the frozen mud in his nightclothes and wellingtons. Richard called to Gordon, who whistled for Juliette. She came running over, pushed past Richard and with her torch beam jiggering wildly over the frosty earth she got to the boy first, shaking him by the shoulders and berating him for leaving the house. The others watched as she lifted him on to her hip and brought him back up to the lane.

In the light of the various torch beams, Ewan's eyes looked strange and stranger still when they returned to the house. Even in the hallway, his pupils remained so dilated that barely any of the colour showed.

'Has he been sleepwalking?' said Gordon.

It didn't appear so. Ewan didn't have the vacancy of someone in a trance but scrutinised each face with cold intent.

Doug came down the stairs finishing his drink and put his hand on Juliette's cheek.

'Ah, you've found him then,' he said. 'You see. No harm done.'

That seemed to be true at first, but as they took Ewan into the kitchen, Eileen noticed that his skin had turned a deep pink colour. And when Juliette took off his pyjama top, his whole torso was the same.

'What is it? A rash or something?' said Gordon.

Russell put on his glasses and inspected Ewan's neck.

'It might be,' he said. 'If he's been in the wood, then he could have come into contact with something he's allergic to.'

'Like what?' Juliette said, thumbing away Ewan's hair to examine his brow. 'He's been in the wood a hundred times and never come out looking like this.'

'I'm not even sure it is a rash,' said Russell. 'A rash would be blotchy. This looks like sunburn.'

'How can it be sunburn?' Eileen said and took over his position. 'He's just chapped from being outside.'

But when she put the back of her hand on his arm, she found him warm to the touch.

'He could have a virus,' suggested Russell. 'That might account for his eyes.'

'Don't you feel well?' said Juliette, turning Ewan's face to hers.

The boy gazed at her dumbly.

'Are you sure he's not still asleep?' said Gordon and he clicked his fingers close to Ewan's ear.

'Ewan?' Juliette said. 'It's Mummy. Are you all right?'

'Just put him back to bed,' said Doug. 'The poor wee man doesn't need you lot making a fuss over him. Let him sleep. He'll be fine.'

172

'Look at him for God's sake,' Eileen snapped. 'He needs a doctor.'

'What's that he's got in his hand?' said Gordon.

No one had noticed until now that Ewan had a tight hold of something that had stained his wrist and fingertips red.

'Come on,' Richard said. 'Let's see. Did you find something in the field?'

'Can Mummy have it?' said Juliette. 'Show Mummy what it is, Ewan.'

'Didn't you hear?' Eileen said sharply, trying to prise the boy's fingers apart. 'Do as you're told.'

But the more she wrestled with him, the stronger his grip became. Eventually, he crushed what he'd been holding and blood seeped out between his knuckles.

'What is it?' Juliette said, crying now as Ewan relented and loosened his hand. 'What did you do?'

His palm dripped with the pap of some animal's viscera. But as Richard lifted him to the sink and Juliette washed his fingers they could see that most of the blood was his own. Stuck into his skin were small, sharp bones. Ribs. A spine. It was then that the boy began to speak. He still wasn't fully conscious and the narrative was somewhat garbled and frenetic but Richard managed to pick out that Jack Grey had told

Ewan to come to the wood, that he'd show him how to see in the dark and sit very still and catch mice with his bare hands.

~

Yes, thought Richard, he remembered all that clearly enough. He didn't need to be reminded about it by Gordon. Nor did he want to hear his specious interpretations about what had happened that night, especially since it was his stories that had disturbed the boy's sleep in the first place. The man was obsessive. He always had been, about one thing or another; that was just the way he was. But whereas his dogmatism had once been good-natured, this felt intrusive. It truly offended him that Richard could doubt his explanation of why Ewan changed. The arrogance of the man was startling.

The truth of the matter was that after his foray into the wood on New Year's Eve, Ewan had woken the next day sniffling and sneezing, but his usual self. His skin was normal, and he had no recollection of having wandered out of the house the night before. In the sobriety of the morning, the diagnosis was much clearer: the boy had simply had a fever; he'd been half asleep and gone out to play unaware of the time; he'd found the detritus of some dead thing in the wood and picked it up not knowing what it really was. The explanation was simple if Gordon chose to see it.

Richard listened to the sound of his van getting fainter as he walked down the field to the tent. The green smell of damp and leaves and uncoiling ferns that he'd enjoyed on that first spring evening became stronger the closer he came to the wood. He wondered whether the hare might venture out from the undergrowth when dusk fell. There was such stillness here that he might well hear its feet drubbing across the field, though at that moment the thought wasn't particularly pleasant any more. And if it were to come to the tent as the vixen had done, he didn't think that he would like to be trapped with it.

He set up the tripod and with the camera aimed down into the hole he took a dozen photographs from various angles, the flash picking out colours and details that the light of the gas lamp was too soft to show. The root was not entirely black but smeared with deep reds and umbers. A subtle ribbing showed how it had grown as it sniffed out water.

Richard counted the smaller stems that grew from it, some of which were very thin and tapered out like the ends of carrots, but others were more substantial.

In pursuing one particular offshoot that burrowed straight down (how far did it go? Twenty feet? Forty? Fifty?) he came across more. They had to have belonged to the Oak. The abundance was too great for any other explanation. And what he'd found was just a fragment of a great web. If the whole root complex could be somehow mapped, then it might give a more accurate indication of how big the tree itself had been. The mental impression he'd had of it so far seemed, on reflection, much too conservative. After all, one bough had held the weight of three bodies.

Since he'd come across the print of the hanging, the Bonnie Sonnes hadn't been far from his thoughts.

The implication was that if they had swung together then they must have committed their crimes together, and if that were true then it would have devastated the village.

The evidence of that lay partly in the fact that there were no Sayles, Calverts or Beestons left in Stythwaite. Either the families had been hounded out after the hangings or they'd left of their own accord. It was impossible to know. More often than not, the past was left in fragments like this. It was a chip of pottery, a broken skull, a shattered spearhead. Sometimes there was only a handful of words to go on too. Roderick Sayles had 'burned the hay', but whose field he'd set alight had not been recorded. If he'd been hanged in wintertime, then perhaps he'd torched the bales as they sat in storage but why he'd done so was anyone's guess.

And as smoke drifted among the houses and fogged the street, had Edmund Calvert taken the opportunity to go to the church unnoticed? While the other villagers were beating out the fire had he been hitching up his smock in the crypt?

But it was Will Beeston's crime that Richard had contemplated most often. The wood engraver had captured in his face an unmistakable look of joy as he flung the child from the top of the church tower.

If this had been the only thing that had happened, then it would have been logical to conclude that Beeston was just psychotic. But it was unlikely that all three boys had been suffering in that way. It may have been a temporary madness. That was possible. There were berries and plants that grew in the dale even now that could cuff the mind sideways. If not that, if it had been planned, then perhaps they'd made a pact and set out to deliberately torment the village for some reason. Yet their crimes seemed like personal indulgences.

It was no wonder, then, that the boys' fathers had looked to blame it all on Jack Grey. To make the inciter of these offences some fictional sprite of the woods was easier than trying to understand why these lads had suddenly fallen into sin. There was nothing more remote than another person's mind. Even down the bloodline the communiqués were lost. A father had no more chance of truly knowing his son than he had of knowing a stranger. That had been proved to Richard on the day of the spring fair

~

Up until then, things had been relatively peaceful for a few months. Ewan had had no other visitations from Jack Grey. Each school day passed without incident, though the relief Juliette felt as she picked Ewan up at the gates at three only lasted until the following morning when she dropped him off again. He said so little that it was difficult to know what he was thinking. He remained unpredictable and each good day only prolonged the outburst that Juliette (and Richard) sensed was coming. It was apparent that the other parents shared the same apprehension. Not that they said anything.

Since the episode with Susan Drewitt, folk in the village hadn't blanked the Willoughbys as such. No one had forced Juliette to leave the PTA or the Fair Committee, but then no one had insisted she stay either. There was only indifference, which was worse in a way. On the day of the spring fair, they were treated as those from Micklebrow or Lastingly or Skipton were treated: as visitors. It was only the three Burnsall girls who went out of their way to upset the Willoughbys by picking other boys over Ewan as he waited for a turn to ride their pony.

Richard and Juliette were looking at the display of children's artwork when they saw that Ewan was getting frustrated and suggested that he choose something else to do. He complied with less fuss than Richard expected and they went hand in hand to the stall where Audrey Cannon was selling bottles of pop.

For the rest of the afternoon they kept him busy, spinning him on the roundabout, pushing him on the swings, watching him play quoits and skittles, trying to ignore the looks from other parents. Juliette was on edge too but she was determined to show everyone that she was a good, loving mother of a son who could be loved. Richard had to admire her courage, though he knew that it was exhausting her. She was not a natural actress.

The fair always culminated in a game of cricket between those who lived in the village and those who lived on the farms. The Willoughbys, living in neither, sat at the boundary line with the ones too young or too old to play.

Ewan saw that his classmates were kicking a football about by the sycamore trees and he lay on his belly watching them trying to score between the two bicycles they'd let fall into the grass.

'Why don't you go and join in?' said Richard.

'Can I?' said Ewan.

'Of course.'

Juliette looked uncomfortable with the idea but to Richard it seemed like a good opportunity for Ewan to make amends for what had happened with Susan Drewitt.

'Go on,' he said. 'Go and share your lemonade with them.'

Ewan got up and went over to the girls first, offering the bottle. There was a cautious pause and then Susan took it and swigged and passed it around to the others. The football skipped past Ewan's legs and he went after it as the other boys called for him to shoot.

Reconciliation was easy for children of that age, Richard thought. They didn't harbour resentment for long. They weren't afraid. Anger, wariness, jealousy and trepidation were fleeting emotions. It was only as they got older that they turned malicious, like the Burnsall girls who'd come over with the sole intention of taunting Ewan again. Holding the football under his arm, he watched them closely, absorbing the names they called him as they pulled the pony along by its bridle. Sticks and stones, Juliette had taught him. Turn the other cheek.

The girls saw that Richard and Juliette were watching them and moved on, the youngest poking out her tongue as a parting shot. Ewan stared as they went away laughing but was soon distracted when the football was knocked out of his arms and the game resumed.

Juliette rested her head on Richard's shoulder.

'Little bitches,' she said.

Even though he'd told her back in Leeds that it wouldn't be easy to live here, he felt no satisfaction in having it proved. He wanted it to work just as much as her. He wouldn't have agreed to move here at all unless he'd imagined they might be a degree happier. His mother must have felt the same. At least at first.

It was hard to imagine that she hadn't noticed the mood shifting around her in Stythwaite. In fact, he was certain that she had but had chosen to ignore it. Not out of arrogance but because she didn't want to admit that she'd made a mistake. She didn't want to feel like a fool and so she'd blundered on. In her own way, Juliette was doing the same thing.

Drained from the effort of her performance her breaths lengthened against his. She had her eyes closed. Her hand was limp. Richard was weary too. He lay back, taking Juliette with him, allowing her to curl into his side, enjoying the weight of her head on his chest. He shut his eyes against the sunlight and idly teased the stem of a dandelion. The woodpigeons in the sycamores, the warmth of the breeze and the smell of the grass faded as he balanced on the verge of sleep. It was a pleasant vertigo, a welcome unsteadiness. But he slipped and woke at the same moment, everything so much louder as he came to consciousness. Juliette surfaced too and worked the heels of her hands against her temples.

Behind them, the voices of the children were so alike, all melded into shouts and shrieks and laughter, that they didn't notice that Ewan had disappeared until one of the Burnsall girls came running from the wall of the churchyard calling for her father.

He was at the crease with the bat poised and, distracted by his daughter, he let the ball clatter into the stumps. A few people, who hadn't noticed the girl shouting, cheered and clapped but it became obvious to them that something was wrong.

Teddy Burnsall handed the bat to Sam Westbury and followed his daughter over to where the pony had been tied to a tree. The two other girls were there now, bawling at Ewan who squatted down in the grass ignoring them.

Richard and Juliette ran over, parting the crowd that had gathered.

'What's wrong?' said Juliette, putting herself between Ewan and the eldest, Deborah.

'He wants locking up,' she said. 'Little bastard.'

The middle sister harmonised. 'He's not right in the bloody head, that one,' she said and went back to comforting the youngest, who wept and snotted and wanted to go home.

Ewan scraped at the soil with the end of a stick, impervious to the cries of distress.

Behind him, Teddy and Olive Burnsall were trying to calm the pony. Its legs shivered and it shook its bowed head as if it were trying to dislodge flies from its nose. Taking hold of its reins, they managed to turn the animal and lift its chin to see what had happened.

One eye stared at the people standing around, the other had been stabbed to glue.

Ewan hadn't been able to settle that night. Whenever he was on the brink of sleep, he'd snap awake and start to cry. Juliette listened for a while and then rolled over, leaving Richard to see to him, though he had no intention of talking about what had happened until the morning when the incident wouldn't be quite so raw.

Curled on his bed, Ewan had his hands over his ears and it had taken Richard some time to get him to let go.

'What is it you can hear?' he said, holding the boy's head to his chest.

'Jack Grey,' said Ewan quietly.

'He's come back, has he?'

'He was there at the fair.'

'Was he? I didn't see him.'

'You can't see him,' said Ewan. 'He talks, that's all.'

'What's he saying now?' Richard asked.

'He's not saying anything.'

'No?'

'No,' said Ewan. 'Now it's like this.'

He made a strangled sound in his throat.

*

After carrying Ewan down to the study, Richard sat the boy on his knee and they looked through the pictures in the encyclopaedia of birds. Could Daddy make a bird? he asked and handed Richard a sheet of carbon paper. Could Daddy make a rook? And a rook it was, a whole parliament, that became the cast of a story Richard invented while Ewan nestled into his lap.

Once upon a time, he said, willing the incantation to pluck him, Ewan and Juliette out of this life and drop them into another, once upon a time, the rooks came down to Starve Acre and saw that Jack Grey was making a terrible noise in the wood. He was shouting and bellowing and throwing stones at all the birds. So, the rooks waited for Jack to come out into the field and when he did they swooped down and carried him off in their claws. Over the fells they went and across the sea and then . . .

Ewan had fallen asleep against his chest and was breathing deeply. In his hand he clutched one of the paper birds and it was still there when Richard laid him down in his bed. It was hard to reconcile this vulnerable little boy with the cold-eyed creature they'd hurried back to the car that afternoon. For him to have hurt the pony as brutally as he had, to have been so exacting with the stick, hardly seemed possible.

Juliette would want to take him back to see Ellis and Richard knew that he'd have no choice but to let her. Ewan wasn't going to get better on his own. They ought to have acted sooner. That at least was clear. Richard blamed himself. He'd put too much faith in Ewan's behaviour being a natural phase and been too certain that the boy could be taught right from wrong like any other child. Now he had to admit that he had no idea what to do. He should have listened to Juliette. His concession about Ellis would be his apology to her for not doing so. In the morning he'd agree to whatever she wanted. She'd know what to do. Despite what had happened she would still be more able than him to think through the problem rationally. But when he returned to the bedroom and was hanging his dressing gown on the back of the door, she said, 'I'm frightened of him, Richard.' And he believed her.

～

Bad weather rumbled through the dale and Richard closed up the tent and took the camera back to the house. Coming in through the front door, he was about to go up to the study when Harrie collared him.

'Oh, Richard, you tell her,' she said, trying to stop the dog under her arm from barking. 'She won't listen to me.'

He followed her into the kitchen where Juliette was sitting on a chair by the woodstove.

On her lap was the hare.

It lay still while she stroked it from head to haunches, drawing its ears through her fist. The dog's presence didn't appear to faze it at all.

'Get her to take the bloody thing outside, will you?' said Harrie.

'I think you should, Juliette,' said Richard.

'Why?'

'For one thing it stinks,' said Harrie. 'And Cass isn't going to stop making a fuss until you do.'

'Where did you find it?' said Richard.

'You were in the garden, weren't you?' Juliette said, nuzzling the hare's fur with the back of her hand. 'He came to the door of the shed while I was getting more paint.'

'You can't have it in the house,' said Richard.

'That's what I told her,' said Harrie, and moved behind the table away from the hare. 'It's a wild animal.'

'He doesn't look wild to me,' said Juliette.

Under her touch, the hare closed its eyes in contentment.

'It could be ill,' said Harrie. 'They don't normally sit so still, do they? It might be diseased.'

'He's not ill,' Juliette said. 'He's just hungry. Is there anything we can give him to eat?'

'Don't feed it,' said Harrie, muffling the dog's jaws. 'Otherwise you'll never get rid of it. Once it knows that there's food here, it'll keep coming back.'

'Harrie's right,' said Richard. 'Better let it fend for itself. Do you want me to take it outside?'

Juliette looked up at him for the first time since he'd come in and put a protective hand on the hare's back.

'He's wet and cold.'

'Jules, please,' said Harrie. 'Cass is giving me a headache.'

Richard gestured for the animal again and Juliette said, 'No. Let me. I'll do it.'

She stood up and gathered the hare in her arms. Its long legs scrabbled and Harrie moved back even further as Juliette carried it out through the door.

'She was always the same when we were children,' she said, watching her sister walking over to the greenhouse in the rain. 'She was forever bringing in cats and mice and insects. Mostly because she knew I didn't like them.'

By the cherry tree, Juliette stopped and seemed to be talking to the hare, showing it the house, the garden.

'Oh, put it down, Jules, for God's sake,' murmured Harrie.

Eventually, Juliette crouched and unlatched the animal's claws from her shirt and sent it away into the undergrowth.

Richard wondered if it had come back to the house for the same reason the vixen had come back to the tent. There was food here. There was shelter. But the hare had seemed so eager to get away from Starve Acre that it was odd it should return so soon.

'We should start on the second coat now,' said Harrie as Juliette came inside.

'Second coat?' Juliette looked behind her to see where the hare had gone.

'In the nursery,' said Harrie.

'Fine, yes, all right,' Juliette said and peered through the kitchen window as Harrie ushered her back upstairs to carry on painting.

'Bring the cans, Richard, will you?' she said.

Picking up the tins of emulsion, he followed them, leaving Cass to bark at the back door until she was certain that the hare had gone.

~

Richard heard the dog again early that evening, yelping and whining. Then Harrie crying out for help.

Crossing the landing, Richard found her kneeling on the floor of her room stroking Cass's twitching body. Blood had been thrown everywhere, against the walls, the rug, the lampshade by the bed.

'My God, what happened?' said Richard.

'The hare was in here,' said Harrie, holding together what was left of the little dog. 'I tried to chase it off.'

Her hands were scratched and bleeding too.

'Where is it now?' said Richard.

'I don't know, do I? It ran away into the house somewhere. Juliette's gone looking for it.'

'Stay here,' he said.

He closed the door tightly behind him and heard the ticker ticker of the hare's claws as it lopped across the floorboards to the head of the stairs.

Richard started after it and the hare bolted down to the hallway, its hind legs kicking out as it gained speed. At the bottom of the stairs it tumbled under its own momentum, rolling into the telephone table and upsetting the ashtray. Coated in dust, it scratched frantically on the floor until it righted itself. By the time Richard made it down, it was already dashing headlong through the kitchen, where it mounted the table then the draining board before finding the half-open window above the sink. Bending through the gap, it lifted one back leg and then the other over the stay and Richard heard it drop down on to the dustbin lid outside.

Juliette was there in the garden and seeing the hare she smiled and beckoned to it. The animal hob-hobbed through the grass and Juliette picked it up.

She came into the kitchen, wiping the blood off its claws and snout. Her voice had been pitched on a reassuring note but changed when she saw Richard.

'What did you do to him?' she said.

'Don't bring it in here, Juliette.'

'I said what did you do to him?'

'That's Cass's blood,' Richard replied. 'That thing ripped her to pieces.'

'Well, the dog must have provoked him,' said Juliette, moving to the kitchen door.

'I thought you'd let it go.'

'He came back, didn't he?'

Richard held her arm. The hare examined him with its unblinking eyes.

'Put it outside,' he said.

'He's cold and he's hungry. I'm not turfing him out into the dark.'

'It's a nocturnal animal,' Richard said. 'I think it'll survive. Take it to the garden.'

She pulled away from him.

'Give it to me, then,' he said. 'I'll do it.'

'Don't you fucking touch him.' Juliette's raised voice echoed against the ceiling.

She pushed past him to the hallway, meeting Harrie at the foot of the stairs. They began to argue and Richard went to stop things from getting out of hand.

'What am I supposed to tell Shona when I get home?' Harrie was saying. 'Cass is dead.'

'I don't suppose she'll even notice,' said Juliette.

'What's that supposed to mean?'

'You know what I mean.'

Harrie looked to Richard.

'Please get rid of it,' he said. 'At least take it into the scullery. I'll put down some straw or something.'

'Would you want to sleep in the scullery?' Juliette said.

'Look at me for fuck's sake,' said Harrie, showing Juliette her bloodied hands and blouse. 'Look at what it's done.'

'He was only defending himself.'

'From Cass?' said Harrie. 'She's half the size of that thing.'

The hare wriggled in Juliette's arms and she started up the stairs to the top floor, followed by Richard.

'You were doing so well,' said Harrie, going after her too. 'You were better, Jules.'

'Christ,' Juliette said. 'Don't you ever stop talking? It's all you ever do.'

'Don't be like that. I'm only trying to help.'

'No one asked you to interfere.'

'I'm sure that's not why she came, Juliette,' said Richard.

'Don't give me that,' Juliette shot back. 'You didn't want her to be here either.'

'Listen, Jules, why don't you come home to Edinburgh with me?' said Harrie. 'Come and stay with us, or with Mum and Dad. Some time away from here will do you the world of good.'

At the door to the nursery, Juliette covered one of her ears.

'Enough,' she said. 'Just stop.'

193

'No,' said Harrie. 'I'm not going to give up, Jules. You have to talk. You can't keep all of this in your head.'

'Nag nag nag,' said Juliette. 'Didn't Rod manage to knock that out of you?'

Harrie looked at her and eventually said, 'You need help. You really do.'

Richard led Harrie away and Juliette went into the room with the hare over her shoulder.

'I can't stand it,' said Harrie. 'What the hell is wrong with her?'

'I'll speak to her again in the morning,' said Richard.

Harrie opened her palms and looked down at the bib of blood on her chest.

'Go and wash,' said Richard. 'I'll take Cass away. I'll bury her.'

But Harrie was staring past him, shaking her head.

When he turned to look, Juliette was laying the hare in the cot.

She stroked its back and ears, then, seeing that Richard and Harrie were watching her, she closed the door and locked it.

Fetching one of the wooden crates he'd used to trap the hare, Richard went to the guest room and found that Harrie had draped a pillowcase over the dog's body. Blood had seeped through the blue cotton like oil stains.

He lifted the bundle into the box and then carried the box out to the garden. A soft drizzle was falling and in the light from the kitchen window he dug a hole by the greenhouse.

On the lane, he heard Sam Westbury going past in his truck and wondered if he had any expertise when it came to hares. He surely had to deal with them in his hayfield. He'd know how to trap them. Or better still, how to kill them. It seemed the only recourse now, the animal being so aggressive. If it could be chased out of the house and into the glare of a shotgun . . . But perhaps it was best to do it well away from Juliette. Quietly. A snare in the wood or something. Though he suspected the hare would be too shrewd to be snagged like that.

With the pit deep enough, he stabbed the spade into the soil and rolled Cass out of the wooden box. Her injuries were obvious as she tumbled free of her shroud. The hare had ripped open her belly, and almost severed one leg.

~

Just after midnight, the phone rang twice in the hall-way but as Richard came to the top of the stairs, Harrie had already picked it up.

'Yes, it's me, Osman,' she said, wedging the receiver between her ear and her shoulder to light a cigarette. 'Thanks for calling back . . . Yes, I know what time it is . . . Yes, I appreciate that . . . I'm sorry, I didn't know . . . No, I can't speak up . . . Well, why do you think I can't?'

She took a drag and breathed out a curl of smoke.

'No,' she said, 'things are not all right. That's why I wanted to speak to you . . . Well, I'd say it was urgent . . . Look, I can't get her to leave the house . . . You'll have to come here . . .

'Well, no,' said Harrie, tapping off the beak of ash. 'She hasn't agreed to see you as such. But then she's hardly thinking sensibly, is she? . . . No, no, fuck getting her consent, we'll all be dead and buried by then. *I'm* asking you to come . . . I'm her sister, isn't that enough? . . . I'm not being aggressive . . . Yes, yes I know it's late . . . But, she's so unwell, Osman. It's breaking my heart to see her like this . . . I don't know what those bloody people said to her the other night . . .'

She drew on her cigarette and then wiped her eyes.

'What if you were to come as a guest, not as a doctor? Then it would be a social visit, not a consultation . . .

of course there would be a difference . . . Yes, I know you'd need to be invited first, I'll talk to Richard about it . . . Look, you did say you'd help, didn't you? . . . Then why are you being so evasive?'

Harrie listened for some time, letting the cigarette smoulder between her fingers.

'Just get to the point, Osman,' she said. 'Will you come or not?'

The answer was obviously curt.

'Is that can't or won't?' said Harrie and put the phone down.

After sitting for a moment she squashed her cigarette into the ashtray.

'I take it you heard all that?' she said, knowing that Richard was there. 'You must be pleased.'

Richard went down to the hallway. Harrie's knuckles and wrists were hashed with scratches from the hare's claws.

'Aren't they sore?' he said.

Harrie looked at him. 'Don't change the subject, Richard. I want to know why you were listening to a private phone call.'

'It can't have been that private if you took it in the hallway,' he said, holding her hand to examine the injuries more closely.

197

The cuts across the base of her thumb were still weeping and she tightened her lips with the pain.

'I should drive you down to see the doctor,' said Richard. 'You don't want them infected.'

'I'm more than capable of washing my own hands,' she said.

'Yes, but you need something on the wounds. There's probably some iodine in the bathroom.'

He let go and she inspected the lacerations herself.

'I've never seen an animal be that fierce before,' she said. 'I just couldn't stop it. It was so strong.'

'It was probably just frightened,' said Richard.

'No,' said Harrie. 'It came looking for Cass.'

'Why would it do that?'

'I'm just telling you what happened, Richard.'

'Cass didn't go for it first?'

'Of course not. She was terrified. She didn't know what was going on.'

Angry and exhausted, Harrie shook another cigarette from the packet and lit up. Even though she'd cleaned her hands, there was still blood in her hair and behind her ear.

'I'll get it out of the house,' said Richard. 'I'll make sure I take it well away so that it doesn't come back.'

'You'll kill it?'

'Yes. I suppose so.'

'How?' said Harrie. 'Juliette won't open the door.'

'Things just got heated,' Richard said. 'She'll come round.'

'I don't think so. You saw the look in her eyes.'

Richard turned back up the stairs. 'Let me go and speak to her then,' he said.

'She won't listen. Not here. Not while she's obsessing over that animal. She needs proper care, Richard.'

'In a hospital?'

'Is there any other choice now?'

He left her smoking and climbed to the upper floor, switching on the lights as he went. At the door of the nursery he spoke Juliette's name, but his pleas were drowned out by the sound of the cradle rocking on the floorboards. He tried the handle. He beat the flat of his hand against the wood. In response, Juliette switched on Ewan's old record player and Richard paused to listen, trying to work out when she had retrieved it from the boxes in the scullery. Or, rather, how. She'd been barely out of Harrie's sight all day. It had to have been taken opportunistically. It wasn't in her nature to be devious. She'd had a moment of weakness, that was all, and Richard knew that she would be punishing herself for re-opening Ewan's life.

'I only want to know that you're all right,' he said.

But she turned up the volume on 'Who Killed Cock Robin?' until the voice and piano buckled into noise.

Richard waited, rattled the handle once more, and then went down to the study. In the hallway, he heard Harrie ringing Osman again. There was little point. Even if he could be persuaded to speak to Juliette, it was hard to see what difference he'd make.

The psychiatrist his mother had summoned to Starve Acre when his father's behaviour could no longer be passed off as tiredness or eccentricity had made at least half a dozen visits at thirty pounds a time and got nowhere. It had been the same at Brackenburn too. The problem was that his father didn't think that there was anything wrong with him. So what use was a cure for a man who wasn't ill? It would be like trying to put out an unlit fire.

Even after – what was it now? – eleven or twelve years since his father had passed on it was still easy to picture Brackenburn, with its smell of mop buckets and kitchens and the long corridors like cloisters. There was always someone wailing somewhere. The nurses always running.

In the room where Richard's father had died and his mind had finally switched off, there'd been nothing but a wooden table and starched sheets. A subtle bar across the window.

There had to be something better for Juliette than that.

Richard had begun to think that Harrie was right. It was doing Juliette no good being here at Starve Acre. She did need to get away. Not back to her family but to some neutral ground where she might be able to think more clearly. Perhaps Stella might put them up for a few days and give them some space. The more the idea coalesced, the more crucial it seemed to extract Juliette from the house as soon as he could.

~

The following afternoon, Richard heard Harrie making her way up the stairs to the study. She didn't knock.

'It's Juliette,' she said, beckoning him out of his seat. 'She's gone. She's taken Ewan's old pram. It's not in the scullery.'

They went on to the lane and looked in both directions. Richard called for Juliette and got nothing back.

'Will she have gone down to the village?' said Harrie.

Another call and more silence.

'Where did she used to walk with Ewan? To the grocer's? She won't have gone to your friend's house, will she?'

Richard didn't think so but Harrie still persuaded him to phone Gordon, who offered to go and look for her in the van straight away.

'And if I find her?' he said.

'Just call the house,' said Richard. 'Harrie will be here.'

But by the time he'd hung up she was already out of the door and fishing her keys from her pocket. Richard got into the Austin's passenger seat and Harrie started the engine at the third attempt.

From the drive, she turned left and followed the lane as it ran along the edge of the moor. After a while, it swung into the lonelier heartland, where it rose and fell and eventually dropped down into Micklebrow some three miles further on.

Ewan had always enjoyed playing the guide when- ever they walked here. He liked to trace their progress on the Ordnance Survey sheet with his finger, delighted that the symbols matched what he could actually see; that he, Mummy and Daddy could be there in real life and in the world of the paper map at the same time. He never made it all the way to Micklebrow on foot, however, even though he protested that he could. After a mile or so he began to drag his heels and they'd stop to rest at the Siblings.

The four erratic boulders were balanced on an outcrop of limestone and though Richard had explained to Ewan how they'd got there – how they'd been inched down from Ribblehead by the glaciers thirteen thousand years ago – the boy preferred the story that Gordon had told him. That these mossy Silurian blocks were really the sons and daughters of a widower who, terrified of losing them as he had his wife, had found some means to turn them into stone and preserve them for eternity. The logic was untidy, but that didn't matter. If you put your ear to the rock you could hear them talking. If you left a flower in one of the cracks it would be gone the next day. No, not eaten by sheep or whipped away by the wind but taken as a gift from one living child to another.

The others in Ewan's class teased him for believing such a tale and he couldn't understand why. Juliette explained that they were just being mean, that they were making fun of him because they couldn't think of anything better to do. But it wasn't unusual, Dr Monk had told them at the clinic, for some children to have difficulty separating the imaginary from the actual. They couldn't choose. To them, everything was real.

It had been Ellis who'd made the appointment for them with Monk. He hadn't been able to speak highly enough of her. Juliette had been much relieved to know that there was someone who might be able to help them, and Richard had been glad to see her smile again. But, they ought not to have gone. They should have known before they got there how Ewan would be. He hadn't bought any of their lies about where they were going and why, and by the time they arrived he'd been tense and reluctant.

She'd seen it all before, though, Monk, and when she called them from the waiting room into her office she merely noted Ewan's opposition and asked her colleague to take him into the soft toy playroom along the corridor while she spoke to Mr and Mrs Willoughby.

She was hawk-nosed, greying, with cheeks of broken veins and would have probably been quite intimidating to children if not for a kindliness in her eyes.

'Mummy and Daddy won't be long,' she said. 'You'll not be far away.' And with glum resignation the boy sloped off behind the nurse.

Juliette did most of the talking as Monk took down Ewan's case history, recalling everything that had happened over the previous year and coming eventually to the Burnsalls' pony.

'He said that someone told him to do it,' Juliette added.

'Another child?' said Monk, looking up with her pen poised.

'No, someone he'd imagined,' said Juliette. 'Someone called Jack Grey.'

Monk nodded.

'He's convinced the voice is real,' Juliette insisted.

'That's not uncommon.'

'You've treated children like Ewan before, then?' asked Richard.

'I've treated plenty of children who've had auditory hallucinations,' said Monk, capping her pen with exactness. 'But whether that's what's happening with Ewan is another matter.'

'But it must be,' said Juliette.

'I know that seems like the logical answer,' Monk replied. 'But I'd have to spend some time with Ewan before I was able to make a diagnosis like that. And it may be that I can't.'

'How do you mean?' Juliette said.

'Well, it could turn out that there is no condition for me to diagnose, Mrs Willoughby.'

'But it's all there,' said Juliette looking at Monk's notebook. 'You can't tell me there's nothing wrong with him. That isn't normal behaviour for a five-year-old.'

Monk smiled at her. 'I have to be very sure,' she said, 'before I attach a label to a child. It's not something I aim for.'

'How much time?' asked Juliette.

'I'm sorry?'

'How much time will you need with him? Weeks? Months?'

Frowning a little, Monk said, 'That's not something I can tell you just yet, I'm afraid. I'll speak to him today, of course, and perhaps I might be able to give you some idea after that.'

'We're just concerned about him missing school,' said Richard.

'You've removed him from the one he was attending, have you?' said Monk, leafing back through her notes.

'We had no choice,' said Juliette, and Richard concurred.

The head had tried to persuade them to let Ewan stay but when they'd asked her how he could possibly sit in a class full of farmers' children day in day out after what he'd done, she didn't have an answer.

'Well, I'm sure that a short break won't do him any harm,' said Monk. 'And it might be that a new school will make a big difference to his behaviour. It does happen.'

'So, we can look for somewhere else?' said Juliette.

'Of course you can.'

'A normal school?'

'Yes,' said Monk, 'a normal school.'

'But will they take him? Given the way he is?'

Monk thought for a moment and looked at them both. 'What we need to do,' she said, 'is to try and ascertain whether his aggression is likely to flare up again in the future. And the way to do that is to work out what it is that triggers these episodes in the first place.'

'Ewan's not aggressive,' said Juliette.

She saw that Monk was re-reading the account of the spring fair.

'What I mean is, he shouldn't be,' Juliette continued. 'Richard and I aren't like that. Ewan's just unwell.'

'Tell me when you think it began,' said Monk. 'Was it when he started school, or before?'

'It was school for sure. He was never like this before he went to Holy Cross,' said Juliette.

'He gave you no cause for concern at all?'

'Not in this way, no.'

'Does he have friends?'

'Not as such.'

'What about when he was at nursery school? Did he play with the other children there?'

'Sometimes. When he could. He wasn't quite as far on as they were. He was born prematurely, as I said.'

'He found his own games to play?'

Juliette put her hand flat on the table. 'Look, I know where you're going with this – that he was lonely and made up a friend in his head.'

'It is a possibility,' said Monk.

'But the voice he hears isn't friendly,' Richard said. 'It terrifies him.'

'All children have the capability to make fantasies seem very real,' said Monk.

'Some more than others, though?' Juliette said.

'There are children who are genuinely confused between the two, yes,' said Monk.

'That's Ewan, then.'

'Again, it might seem the case, Mrs Willoughby, but we really need to try and understand how this voice seems to him. Whether it sounds as if it's coming from outside or if it is just an echo in his imagination. You said yourself, Mr Willoughby, that your friend told Ewan stories about this Jack Grey.'

'Does it matter how the voice got into his head?' Richard said. 'Surely the important thing is that we get it out.'

'In which case we need to get to the root of Ewan's unhappiness.'

'What can he possibly be unhappy about?' said Juliette. 'We give him everything.'

'It's nothing to do with what he has, unfortunately,' Monk replied. 'If it were, then it would make my job very simple. It's to do with how he feels. Those are two very different things.'

'Aren't they connected at all?'

'Not so directly as you might think.'

'And will Ewan need medication?'

'Pardon?'

'If you diagnose him with something, will he need to take pills?'

'Mrs Willoughby,' said Monk. 'That's a long way down the road. I can't possibly say. Hopefully not.'

'Do you have any answers?' Juliette said.

Calmly, Monk replied, 'It'll take time. But I'm sure we'll get there.'

'I thought you were going to help us.'

'That's exactly what I'm hoping to do.'

'Then why aren't you listening to me?' Juliette said. 'I've told you everything. Now, you tell me what the matter is with my son.'

She began to sob, brushing off Richard's hand as he insisted that they just had to be patient. Monk took her outburst as equably as she'd taken the glare of resentment Ewan had given her earlier and got up to fetch Juliette a glass of water from the cooler outside in the corridor. She left the door of the office open and carried on talking as she filled the tumbler, though Juliette wasn't listening and neither was Richard.

The place reminded him of Brackenburn. Behind the yellow paint it was damp-marked and peeling. Everywhere had the wet carpet smell of an institution. The rooms were too big. There were always traces of other conversations in the air. Voices carried, especially Ewan's.

Even separated by two doors, they'd heard him crying – no, screaming for them to come. Juliette left Monk's office with Richard, found the playroom, and ignoring the nurse she hitched Ewan on to her hip and carried him away. Monk came after them, insisting that it wasn't unusual for a child to react that way in a strange environment, and if they'd just let him calm down then . . .

The double doors out to the car park cut off her voice.

'What did she say to you, Ewan?' said Juliette. 'What's wrong?'

All the way out of the town, she asked the same questions.

'What did the nurse do to make you so upset? What were you talking about? Wasn't she a nice lady?'

'It wasn't a lady talking,' Ewan finally answered. 'It was Jack Grey.'

~

Once past the rocks, Harrie sped up again, descending into a wide basin of heather and bogland. The country here was open and bleak and much of the winter snow remained, forcing the Drewitts' sheep to eat from the manger of straw at the side of the road. Another bank of cloud brought hail and sleet which collected on the wipers in bars of freezing slush. Harrie shuffled forward in her seat wiping the fogged-up windscreen with her sleeve and peering along the lane which unspooled like a grey ribbon through the moor.

'There she is,' said Harrie, spotting Juliette a quarter of a mile ahead. 'She must be drenched, the silly cow.'

Accelerating harder, she overtook Juliette and pulled in some yards in front. Richard had been hoping to have the first word but Harrie was too quick and was out before he'd unbuckled his seatbelt.

'Get in the car, Juliette,' she said, taking her elbow. 'I mean it. This is stupid.'

Juliette shrugged her off and steered the pram away.

'Where the hell are you going?' Harrie said.

'Be quiet. I'm trying to get him to sleep,' said Juliette. 'Leave me alone.'

Richard stopped her with a hand on the pram's hood. Inside, the hare lay staring.

'Let us take you home,' he said.

'I don't want to go home. I'm going for a walk,' said Juliette.

Harrie clutched her sleeve. 'Jules, look at the weather.'

'So?' said Juliette. 'I'll only get wet. I'll live.'

'You're miles from the house,' said Richard. 'If Harrie drives you back, we'll be there in ten minutes.'

'What would I do with the pram?' she said. 'Leave it here, I suppose?'

'Yes,' said Harrie. 'And that damn thing with it.'

The hare shuffled and kicked under the blankets and Juliette reached in and covered it up again.

212

'I don't know what you think that is,' said Richard. 'But you have to let it go.'

'Let him go? We invited him to the house, Richard,' she said. 'He's here because we wanted him to be.'

'I knew those fucking people would make things worse,' said Harrie.

'Worse?' Juliette said. 'They made everything clear, Harriet. Everything makes sense now. I'm happy.'

Another swell of icy rain swept over the moors.

'If you don't want it to catch cold,' said Richard, watching Juliette tucking the hare in tighter. 'Then I suggest you come back with us now.'

Juliette turned, poised to fight him off. 'Don't pretend you're concerned for him. I know what you'll do,' she said. 'You and her.'

'Juliette, please.'

She pushed away his hand and carried on along the road with her head down against the weather.

Harrie got back into the car and Richard joined her, sopping and numb, his trousers plastered to his legs.

'We should follow her,' said Harrie.

'She won't listen to you.'

'So, what do we do, wait here?'

'I don't know,' said Richard. 'I really don't.'

Short of physically dragging her into Harrie's car, there seemed to be no option but to leave her to go where she wanted.

Harrie switched on the wipers again and said, 'I'm going to have to call Mum and Dad.'

Richard didn't reply and she took this as disapproval.

'Look, we need their help,' she said. 'Osman won't come here, and I can't get Juliette to leave. We have to do something, Richard. If we could only get rid of that animal,' she went on, 'that would be a start.'

'Get rid of it how? Like you said, she won't let it out of her sight.'

'I've been thinking,' said Harrie. 'We could lace its food. She'll have to feed it at some point.'

'Lace it with what?'

'Poison,' said Harrie. 'You must have something. You live in the country. Don't you get rats?'

If they had ever bought poison, then Juliette would have insisted on it being kept out of the house away from Ewan's reach, so when they got back to Starve Acre Richard and Harrie went to search the shed. It smelled wonderfully ordinary, of oil and creosote. On the shelves were unopened packets of seeds, plastic flowerpots, bottles of paint-thinner and methylated spirit. All covered in cobwebs and desiccated spiders.

Harrie found a stepladder and Richard went to the far end of the shed where his father had stored bags of bone-meal and bottles of the home-made concoction he used to kill dandelions. Above the workbench, suspended horizontally on a pair of protruding nails, was the fishing net Richard had bought Ewan the summer before in an attempt to turn him into the little Huckleberry Finn Juliette had always pictured.

~

After the way he'd been at the clinic, the thought of having the boy around the house all the time troubled Juliette. It was unlikely that he'd start at a new school before September, if he started anywhere at all. What was she supposed to do until then? She didn't want to be left alone with him.

Richard worked from home for the rest of the summer term and when the holidays came he made sure to take Ewan out of the house as often as he could.

The boy still didn't like going through the field but having the fishing net in his hand seemed to subdue his worries. Or at least his excitement generally outweighed his apprehension. As a further distraction, Richard instigated the ritual of reciting the names of all the freshwater species they could remember as they went hand in hand through the wood, as though by speaking their names they might be charmed into Ewan's net. Then they'd sit by the beck for an hour or more patiently sweeping the mesh through the water. Richard never hurried Ewan. All the complaints they'd made about him at school – that he was idle and petulant – were remedied here. He was gentle too, lifting whatever he caught from the water to his yellow bucket with great care. If only the Burnsalls could see him like this, thought Richard, then they'd understand that he'd simply been unwell on the day of the fair, easily aggravated through no fault of his own. He hadn't intended to hurt their animal at all. If they could come here and see how placid he was, then he liked to think that they'd have some compassion for him.

On a muggy August evening, a week before he would find the boy lifeless in his bed, Richard had taken Ewan down to the wood to see what he could catch. For a while, he'd tried his luck on the pebbled inlet by the willows but only raked up stones from the bottom of the stream. They were pretty enough, though: pieces of marble-sized limestone and quartz.

Ewan selected the roundest and smoothest ones, washed them in the shallows, and wrapped them inside the handkerchief Richard always shoved into his pocket before he left the house.

'Let's try Willoughby Bridge,' said Richard and Ewan smiled because it was him who'd given that name to the tree fallen across the water.

It was a good spot for fishing. The maw of the net could be secreted in the shadow of the trunk and things would swim inside without even realising they'd been caught.

Richard watched him closely. Now that he was away from school, he seemed different. Replaced. And it hurt to think that he'd been so blinded by concern that he was only noticing now that the boy was growing up.

'Look,' said Ewan.

He'd caught some writhing thing in his net. An eel, black and greasy.

'Quick, Daddy, the bucket.'

Richard filled it from the stream and Ewan lowered the eel into the water, where it sprang free, whacking the sides with its tail.

'I'm going to catch another one,' he said and went back to his spot on the bank.

He caught three more in quick succession and sank them into the bucket where they slithered over one another like a knot that was always in the process of being tied.

'Can we take them home?' said Ewan, down on his haunches and studying the creatures intently.

'I think they'd prefer to stay in the beck,' Richard said.

'But I want to show Mummy.'

'I'm not sure Mummy would like eels all that much, do you?'

'She might.'

'Well, perhaps we can persuade her to come and watch you catch them here?'

'But I might not catch anything when she comes.'

'All the same.'

'Can't we take them home and show Mummy and then bring them back?'

'The bucket would be very heavy, Ewan.'

'But I'm strong now.'

Yes, he was. And watching him there in the fluid light of the trees, Richard could, for a moment, imagine what he might look like at ten or sixteen.

In time, when they became a mere moment in the larger pattern of his life, these last twelve months would dwindle in significance and perhaps be forgotten altogether. What Ewan had been didn't have to dictate what he would become.

That thought, above all, had haunted Richard in the weeks after the funeral. Ewan could have been different. He could have been made well. But they had run out of time. And now in other people's eyes, he would always be unredeemed. He would always be a violent little boy.

~

As Richard suspected, there was no poison in the shed but he was sure that Cannon's would have something and promised Harrie that he'd drive down to the village once he'd packed up the tent.

He'd resigned himself to the fact that if Juliette's parents were coming, then they'd be coming to stay, and it would be difficult for him to carry on working in the field. He would be needed in the house, if only to mediate the arguments that would inevitably start as soon as they arrived. Like Harrie, Eileen wouldn't give up until Juliette was away from Starve Acre and in a hospital bed. But Juliette was unlikely to go willingly.

When he went out on to the lane, he watched for her coming back to the house. Ten minutes passed. Fifteen. He waited two more and then headed down to the tent.

In the lamplight, the hole he'd excavated looked even more tangled, as each root was doubled by its shadow.

He had yet to dig out the whole length of the rectangle he'd marked and decided that he would try to unearth the final third of it and photograph what was there before he took down the tent and covered up the site with tarpaulin.

The hole was deep enough for him to crouch in now, and if he carefully stepped between the lattice of stems, he could scrape away at the remaining soil with more control. There was no profit in rushing things. It was better to uncover a little cautiously than to go at it with a shovel just to get finished. Haste caused things to be lost for ever. He'd tell his students that the key was simply to adopt an attitude of respect. Time had a way of fixing things very firmly into the earth and relics often had to be massaged free. Though it was taxing on the fingers, especially here in the field where the mud was as thick as clay in places and came away in greasy lumps that stained his palms.

One particular branch widened the more he scooped away and after another foot or so it connected into a span of wood that ran straight across the plot. As he carved off the dirt, it became clear that this was not one of the roots. It was covered in bark.

He smoothed his hand along its length, peeling away the clotty soil and exposing it a little more with each pass. It was a hulk of a thing, thick and rugose like the trunk of a mammoth. His fingers found deep grooves scored into the meat of it that looked like rope marks. He'd seen them before. When he'd visited Jerusalem as a student, he'd been taken by a dozen different guides to see a dozen different trees, each one, of course, the true place of Judas's suicide.

Unless another giant gallows-tree had grown and died since the Stythwaite Oak stood here, then this had to be Old Justice.

Climbing out of the pit, Richard cleaned his hands on his trousers as much as he could and then moved the camera so that he could photograph what he'd found. If this was the hanging bough then he could only speculate about why it was here. If it had simply fallen or been cut down then it would have decayed in the field. It was possible that it had sunk into soft mud and gradually been swallowed up by the earth, but it seemed much more likely that it had been deliberately buried. Perhaps the incidents involving the three boys had been so distressing that all reminders were removed afterwards. Perhaps all traces of legal irregularity too. For it wasn't unknown in those days for lynch mobs to circumvent the work of the assizes, or for a conceited JP to proclaim himself judge, jury and executioner. But whatever the process, the hearing of the boys' transgressions would have been swift and the verdict incontestable. With Jack Grey as their only defence, they would have been laughed out of the dock and strung up all the quicker.

~

An hour later, Juliette came back to the house. With the front door wide open, she reversed the pram into the hallway leaving tracks of rainwater and mud along the floor. She was drenched, her face ruddy with the cold. But the hare was her only concern and she lifted it out from the blankets and rubbed its fur.

'Mum and Dad are on their way,' said Harrie, standing next to Richard in the doorway of the kitchen. 'I'm going to collect them from the station this evening.'

Juliette ignored her and, still in her raincoat, she carried the hare upstairs.

'You can lock yourself away in that room if you like,' said Harrie, moving to the newell post. 'But Dad will break the door down if he has to. He'll wring that animal's bastard neck too. You know he will.'

She shouted Juliette's name up the stairwell but decided against pursuing her and took her frustration out on Richard instead.

'Aren't you going to the village?' she said.

Thankfully, it was Neville Cannon on the counter rather than his wife. If Audrey had been serving, then Richard would have been stuck there for half an hour while she asked about Juliette and how things were at the house and if she would be going back to work, before passing on her wisdom about the eradication of rats. Neville, on the other hand, liked to spend as little time with customers as possible and exchanged the box of poison pellets for Richard's money with only a brief nod.

On his way out of the shop, Richard watched Gordon coming along the street in his van. He flashed his lights and stopped behind Richard's car.

'Please tell me you've found her,' he said, unrolling the window and leaning out. 'I've been going up and down the dale for hours.'

Having been sent out so abruptly by Harrie and consumed with the thought of what would happen

223

when Eileen and Doug appeared at Starve Acre, it had slipped Richard's mind to let Gordon know that Juliette had come back home.

'I should have phoned you,' he said. 'I'm sorry.'

'There's no need to apologise. I just hope she's all right.'

'She's fine.'

He noticed what Richard was carrying. 'Problems?' he said.

'I think there's a nest in the garden,' said Richard.

Gordon looked doubtful. 'Why don't you come to the house,' he said. 'I've hardly seen you in days.'

'Another time,' said Richard. 'Juliette's parents are coming. I need to get back home.'

'Her parents?' Gordon said. 'What for?'

'Parents do visit their children from time to time.'

'Tell them not to come. No one should be in that house.'

Richard moved away towards the car.

'I'm not interested in Mrs Forde's stories,' he said.

'Whatever's wrong at Starve Acre,' said Gordon, eyeing the packet in Richard's hand again, 'it's not Mrs Forde's doing.'

'If you say so,' Richard replied, trying to work out if there was enough room to reverse past the van.

'Let me talk to you,' Gordon said.

'I told you, I need to get back.'

'A few minutes, Richard. You can spare me that, can't you?'

He held the passenger door open and after hesitating for a moment Richard climbed in and sat next to him.

His wool suit smelled damp, and there was a little sweet alcohol on his breath.

'I know you've found something in the field,' said Gordon and held up his hand to cut short Richard's insistence that he hadn't. 'And I know that you won't tell me the truth about it. I don't want to argue, I want you to listen to me.'

Richard indicated that he was. Stuck in the van, he had no choice.

'After Ewan died,' Gordon said, 'Juliette and I spent a lot of time talking.'

'I know you did,' said Richard.

'And she told me things that she didn't tell anyone else.'

Richard had always suspected that that had been the case. Juliette had never spent hours unfolding her soul to him – but he knew that it was often easier to speak to a stranger, as it were, than someone enveloped in the same grief.

'I don't mean her feelings necessarily,' Gordon said. 'I'm talking about certain facts concerning Ewan.'

'Such as what?'

Richard could see that his shortness was making Gordon uncomfortable and he was both glad and sorry for it.

'This is hard for me,' Gordon said. 'I've known you for a long time. You're a good friend.'

'As are you,' said Richard. 'But this Mrs Forde has caught you, Gordon. And to be honest, I'm surprised; a man of your intelligence.'

'Caught me?'

'Conned you, then.'

Gordon's frustration got the better of him for a moment. 'Do you still think that this is it?' he said. 'What you see or what you can feel under your hands is everything?'

'Of course it is. You're deluded if you think otherwise.'

The hare's transformation had been unnatural but it had required no intellectual sacrifice, no faith, no imagination. It had occurred in this world of forms. For whatever reason it had happened, whatever it meant, it was real.

'Forgive me, Richard,' said Gordon, 'but if you can't

see that Ewan was affected by something in that field, then you're more deluded than anyone.'

'It was make-believe,' Richard said. 'From the stories you told him about Jack Grey.'

'I only told him about Jack Grey so that he had a name for what he'd seen or heard. I thought it would make more sense to him.'

'I'm not following you.'

'I'm saying that I don't know what's there, Richard. Not entirely. No one does.'

'Really? I'm shocked.'

'I'm not sure that being facetious is very helpful any more.'

'How else should I be? It's nonsense, Gordon. Like all that drivel the Beacons came out with.'

'I'll excuse your ignorance. You're obviously upset.'

'Come on,' said Richard. 'If there were anything in it, I'd have seen what the rest of you saw when Mrs Forde came to the house. I passed her test, didn't I? She found whatever she needed to find in my blood.'

Gordon turned away from him and looked down the street. He'd rigged it.

'For Christ's sake,' said Richard. 'Why?'

'You wanted to be with Juliette, didn't you?'

'So, it was kindness, was it?'

'Insurance.'

'Sorry?'

'None of us wanted you to sabotage the meeting. It was too important.'

'For who?'

'For Juliette, of course.' Gordon turned to face him square on. 'The guilt was killing her, Richard. I couldn't let her carry on feeling like that.'

'We both felt guilty, Gordon.'

'It was different for her.'

'How?'

Gordon paused then said, 'She was with Ewan when he died, Richard. She let him go.'

Richard looked at him and went to get out but Gordon held his wrist tight until he took his seat again.

'It was for your sake,' he said.

'My sake?'

'I have to tell you this,' Gordon said. 'Please listen.'

'Tell me what?'

Still gripping Richard's arm, Gordon said, 'You don't know how close you came to dying.'

'What are you talking about?'

'I'm talking about Ewan, Richard.'

'Ewan?'

'Juliette told me that she woke one night a few days before he died and saw him standing next to you with a handful of pebbles from the beck,' said Gordon. 'You were fast asleep. You had your mouth open.'

'He wouldn't have done anything.'

'No?'

'It would have been a prank,' said Richard. 'He was only five.'

'But if Juliette hadn't woken up?'

'Then what? Even if he'd tipped the lot in, I'd have spat them out.'

Gordon looked at him. 'No, no, Richard,' he said. 'Ewan had wet the stones so that they'd slip down your throat. You would have choked to death.'

He rubbed his thumb over Richard's knuckles.

'Let me drive you up to Starve Acre,' he said. 'Don't go back on your own.'

'Move your van,' said Richard, opening the door and getting out.

'We could try to persuade Juliette to stay with me and Russell,' Gordon went on. 'I could make room.'

Richard looked at him until he switched on the engine.

~

Where the top road levelled out, Richard put his foot down and cut through the puddles and the trails of mud from the farmers' trucks. Every few seconds he cast his eyes to the rear-view mirror expecting to see Gordon following him. The man was a fool for taking what Juliette had told him at face value. She simply wanted someone to blame for what had happened and so she'd blamed herself. What mother wouldn't? She hadn't watched Ewan die at all. It was a metaphor. She'd been sound asleep when it happened and so in her mind for all the use she'd been that night she might as well have stood by and observed. Gordon knew nothing.

Richard hoped that they had parted with enough hostility to make him stay away, at least for now. Things would be bad enough with Juliette's parents here. Especially her mother. Eileen's heavy-handed-ness would only provoke Juliette into strengthening the barricades.

Still, now that Harrie had set off for the station Juliette would be on her own. If they could only have the chance to talk, he was certain that he'd be able to get through to her. With only the two of them in the house it seemed more likely that she'd listen. And if she were willing to listen, then she might be persuaded to leave.

*

Expecting to find Juliette still holed up in the nursery, he was surprised to hear her moving about in the kitchen. He stashed the box of poison behind the row of wellingtons in the hallway and hung his coat on the rack.

When he went in, she looked up from the table and finished off slicing a sandwich of meat and pickles.

Something about her appearance had changed. There was colour in her face. Her eyes were brighter.

'Are you hungry?' she said. 'I can make you something if you like.'

Richard shook his head and sat down opposite her. He wondered what she'd done with the hare.

'It's good to see you eating again,' he said.

Between mouthfuls, she said, 'It feels like I can't fill myself today. I'm hungry all the time.'

'You've some catching up to do, I suppose.'

He'd always been able to tell when an apology was coming. Juliette would offer her hand in a particular way, beckoning until he took it. She did so now.

'I'm sorry, Richard,' she said.

'For what?' he said. Her skin was so warm. Her pulse kicked against his fingers.

'For going off earlier. I didn't mean to worry you.'

'It doesn't matter. You came back.'

'I know I've been difficult to live with,' she said, and as Richard began to reply, she interrupted with, 'No, don't pretend. I have.'

'It's been hard for all of us,' he said.

'It was only because I didn't understand what was happening. I'm better now.'

She let go of his hand, took another bite of her sandwich and wiped butter from her lip.

Richard looked at the clock. 'How long's Harrie been gone?'

'I don't know.'

'Didn't you hear her leave?'

'I was busy.'

'You do know that she's gone to fetch your parents, don't you?' said Richard.

'Of course.'

'Well, aren't you worried?' he said. 'You know what they want to do.'

'Do I?'

'They'll take you to hospital.'

'And how are they going to do that?' said Juliette. 'Pick me up and throw me in the back of the car?'

'You know what I mean.'

'Richard, none of them can do anything. And once they realise that, they'll go home again.'

'I think you're seriously underestimating your mother, Juliette.'

'It doesn't matter how loud she shouts. She only has words.'

'She'll write letters and make phone calls. She'll bring doctors.'

'This is our house though, isn't it?' said Juliette.

'So?'

'So we don't have to let anyone in that we don't want.'

He made her look at him. 'It might come to the point where none of us has a choice about that any more,' he said.

'I'm not ill, Richard. Perhaps I was, before the Beacons came. But now everything's clear. I don't feel confused.'

'You do know that it was a set-up, don't you?' said Richard. 'Gordon persuaded Mrs Forde to let me stay.'

'I thought that was probably the case.'

'Then how can you believe a word she said?'

'It doesn't matter what she said. It was what she showed me,' said Juliette. 'In fact, I don't even know that it was her who showed me. When I saw how things really are, it didn't feel as though it was anything I didn't already know.'

'That's exactly how Gordon put it.'

'Well, that's how it is,' she said, patiently accepting his cynicism. 'I'm not saying it just because he did.'

'It was a trick, Juliette,' said Richard. 'And a convincing one, I'll give you that. But if you're just clinging on to all this because you're ashamed of being fooled, then there's no need to feel like that. You were desperate.'

She smiled peaceably and looked at him. 'It wasn't a trick and I wasn't fooled.'

He turned to the clock again. 'We could get away,' he said. 'We could pack a few things and leave.'

'Leave? What for? I can't go anywhere, can I?'

'Of course you can. What's stopping you?'

She lifted her eyes to the ceiling. 'He's sleeping,' she said. 'I don't want to wake him yet.'

'They will take it away, you know,' he said.

'They'd have to catch him first.'

'Why don't we let it out in the field?' he said. 'That would be a start. It might just convince them that you're getting better.'

She was smiling at him. She didn't understand.

'Juliette, listen to me,' he said. 'Once your mum and

dad get here, you and I won't be able to talk about this alone any more. Which is why we should go.'

'Talk about what?'

'You. That animal, Juliette. What do you think I mean?'

'We are talking, aren't we?'

'I mean talk properly. Away from here. Where we've got more time.'

'Richard, we've got the rest of our lives. What are you worried about?'

She finished the sandwich and started to quarter an apple with a fruit knife.

'Please, Juliette. Just pack a bag and let's go. Stella would have us for a few days. I'm sure she would.'

'But I'm perfectly happy here.'

'For now, maybe. But everything's going to change. Believe me.'

Juliette drew the knife through the flesh to cut out the pips.

'I feel sorry for you, Richard,' she said. 'I really do. I'd give anything for you to feel at peace. Jesus, when I think of all those months I wasted blaming myself for what I did,' she went on. 'It's no wonder I was ill.'

'For what you did?'

235

'Ewan,' she said. 'I was with him when he was dying. And I did nothing.'

'He died on his own, Juliette. It was the middle of the night.'

'No, I was there too. I woke up and went to him while you were asleep.'

'And you left him in his bed for me to find the next morning? Come on. I don't believe you'd do that.'

Richard held her hand again. 'What happened to Ewan wasn't anyone's fault,' he said. 'Certainly not yours. You mustn't feel guilty.'

'But that's just it,' she said. 'I don't feel guilty any more. I know that the light left him for a reason.'

'What are you talking about?'

'Because he was so unhappy, because he would have carried on hurting people,' she said. 'Richard, there's such an intelligence to everything that happens. I wish you could see it.'

'There wasn't any reason why Ewan died when he did,' said Richard. 'The doctors said so. Don't you remember?'

She offered him a wedge of apple. He said nothing and she ate it herself.

'You'll come to realise how privileged we are soon

enough,' she said. 'We've got another chance to love, Richard.'

'A child, Juliette. Not that animal.'

'But we called him, and he chose to come. That's wonderful, isn't it?'

She touched his hair, kissed him and went out.

He watched her go and soon heard the pipes of the house pink and rattle when she ran the bath taps.

Despite what Juliette said, it was clear that she still felt culpable for the boy's death. But Ewan's heart had been imperfect from birth. Two doctors had told them that. The abnormality could have made itself apparent at any time, they said. He might have been taking his first steps or queuing for his pension. There was no telling. No one could have understood all the contexts and patterns that determined his survival from one moment to the next. Which meant that there was no better way that he could have lived. There was nothing that Richard or Juliette could have done differently.

At the time, it had been no comfort to hear. But it had the benefit of being true. It could be demonstrated with diagrams. There were books that explained a defective heart in great detail.

*

In the study Richard searched for them on the shelves and among the mounds under the window. Down in the hallway, the phone started to ring. Knowing it would be Gordon, he deliberated and then ignored it, peeling off the tape from the last of the cardboard boxes.

He didn't believe that Juliette was so far gone that she couldn't be reasoned with. No one ever fell that far. Even his father might have been brought back, given time.

From the box he took out books on pancreatic cancer, the Iberian lynx, amino acids, the rings of Saturn, fenland irrigation and the ichthyosaurus.

Between a volume on granite and a treatise on pneumatology was a small leather folder and inside the remaining woodblock prints had been sewn together with string. Richard took the book over to the desk and switched on the lamp.

Here were the three boys, the Bonnie Sonnes, being apprehended by the parish mob.

Here they were, shackled in a cell.

Over the page a courtroom of leaded windows and anguished faces, the Justice in his chair compelling the defendants to 'difclofe all facts before God'.

Next, the village-made instruments of persuasion. The blacksmith's tongs. The ploughman's whip.

They had been productive, it seemed, for confessions quickly followed.

''Twas Jack Grey caſt his eye upon us! He bid us do much cruelty, sir!'

'And where dids't thou meet him?' asked the Justice.

The artist had described the answer that came.

Here were the three boys standing in the field by moonlight.

Here were the three boys on their knees, bowing down to the creature coming out of the wood.

A large, bright-eyed hare.

The last few pages of the book were brittle and brown with age and would not stand to be turned too often. Perhaps it was better that way.

Here were the villagers congregated around the tree 'In Gladneſſ Of A Devilment Ended'.

From the bough, the rope hung long and tight, and at its end the hare sagged in the throttle.

Now here was the hangman burying the animal beside the corpses of the three boys.

Here was the forester with his saw in his hand watching the villagers dumping Old Justice into the same grave pit.

Outside, Richard heard Harrie pulling into the driveway. The car juddered for a moment or two and then fell silent. He wished that he'd bolted the front door. That would have bought him some more time with Juliette. Leaving the prints on his desk, he went upstairs to warn her that her parents had arrived and found the door to the nursery unlocked. She was in her dressing gown, still damp from the bath. She invited him in and went back to watching the hare as it started to twitch itself awake under the blankets in the cot.

A night-light held the room in a soft blue glow. A clock ticked. Some more of Ewan's toys had been recovered from the boxes in the scullery and the rug was littered with plastic animals and brightly coloured building blocks, some stacked, some knocked over in fun.

Below, the hallway became loud with talk as Harrie, Eileen and Doug came in. The phone began to ring again.

Richard tried to speak to Juliette but she hushed him and leaned over the bars to pick up the hare. It took some effort. It had grown large and muscular. Its long body dangled and she folded in its wheeling back legs until it rested against her chest.

She had been right. The hare wanted to be here. It had always wanted to be here. When he'd taken it out to the field, it had tried to get back to Starve Acre and find Juliette. It had only run into the wood because he'd forced it that way.

Eileen called out. Richard heard her heels going into the kitchen. Harrie answered the phone and began arguing with Gordon.

'What should I do?' said Richard.

'Let them come,' Juliette said.

'But they can't see you like this.'

Eileen was running up the stairs now, yelling for Juliette again. Doug followed her, shouting louder. But there was no anger in their voices, only a strain of fear that Richard knew well. It was the unique dread of every mother and father. The persistent sense that their children had always been drifting away from them. Out of reach and beyond their help. Into their own deranged worlds.

Sitting in the rocking chair, Juliette set it going with her foot and stroked the animal's ears. When it was settled, she undid the belt of her dressing gown, working her shoulder free and cupping her breast, which had grown engorged and milky white. She offered the nipple to the hare and, with a paw resting on her sternum, it latched tight and drank.

Acknowledgements

Thanks to Nathan Connolly at Dead Ink Books for commissioning the book in the first place and inviting me to be part of the unique Eden Book Society project. Also, everyone at John Murray who has worked so hard to bring the book together – my fabulous editor, Mark Richards, for his continued faith in my writing and to Becky Walsh, Amanda Waters and Morag Lyall for their close attention to detail and all their invaluable advice. Thanks to publicists extraordinaire Yassine Belkacemi and Emma Petfield for their ongoing support in promoting my work. As always, I am indebted to Lucy Luck, my fantastic agent. Thank you for all you do, especially keeping me sane and in gainful employment. Finally, to my beautiful family, Jo, Ben and Tom – thanks for being so understanding when I'm burning the midnight oil out in the shed.

From Byron, Austen and Darwin
to some of the most acclaimed and original
contemporary writing, John Murray takes pride in
bringing you powerful, prizewinning, absorbing
and provocative books that will entertain you
today and become the classics of tomorrow.

We put a lot of time and passion into what we
publish and how we publish it, and we'd like to
hear what you think.

Be part of John Murray – share your views with us at:

www.johnmurray.co.uk

 johnmurraybooks

 @johnmurrays

 johnmurraybooks